RHAPSODY FOR THE TEMPEST

RHAPSODY FOR THE TEMPEST

THE BRAINTRUST™ BOOK 3

MARC STIEGLER

LMBPN Publishing
PMB 196, 2540 South Maryland Pkwy
Las Vegas, NV 89109

First US Edition, August 2018
Version 1.01, October 2018

ISBN: 978-1-64202-064-9

ACKNOWLEDGMENTS

Special thanks this time go to Hugh Hoover for teaching me about keeping your limits open on your homebrew bots; Sheryl Corchnoy who supplied the psych eval; and Dr. James Caplan for his expertise on scenario testing and other matters of education tech.

SHIPS OF THE ARCHIPELAGOS

The BrainTrust's main fleet:

Argus: Manufacturing ship specializing in the manufacture of isle ships, but performing diverse manufacturing tasks including the manufacture of rocket boosters for SpaceR.

BTU: Ship hosting BrainTrust University, also known as BTU.

Chiron: Medical ship catering to medical tourists, i.e., people needing medical care who want to avoid either the long lines or high costs of medical procedures in Western countries.

Dreams Come True: Isle ship filled with startup companies.

Elysian Fields: Tourist ship, also known as 'the Party Boat.'

FB Alpha & Beta: Two of the original four BrainTrust isle ships, mainly hosting FB employees but also leasing space to other companies.

GPlex I & II: Two of the original four BrainTrust isle

ships, mainly hosting GPlex employees but also leasing space to other companies.

GPlex III: GPlex isle ship filled with compute servers.

GS Prime: Goldman Sachs financial services ship, mainly hosting GS employees but also leasing space to other financial services companies.

GSDC: Goldman Sachs Data Center ship.

Haven: Residential isle ship built by billionaires for billionaires.

Heinlein: Modified isle ship used as launch pad for SpaceR rockets. Kept at a safe distance from the main fleet, often moves closer to the equator for launches.

Helios: Manufacturing ship belonging to SpaceR, under construction, intended for the manufacture of Kestrel Titans.

Hephaestus: Factory ship where operations involving toxic and explosive materials take place. Nuclear reactors are built here. The ship is kept at a safe distance from the main archipelago.

Warenhaus: Logistics ship which also contains a silicon chip foundry.

Wells Morgan: Joint venture of Wells Fargo and J.P. Morgan, hosting diverse financial services companies.

The Fuxing fleet/archipelago stationed off the coasts of China, Taiwan, and the Philippines:

Mount Helicon: School and residential ship, with only a skeleton crew until the *Taixue* is well-populated.

Taixue: School and residential ship, the flagship, the

first home of new students, employees, and families from around the South China Sea.

Zhaozhou: Manufacturing ship under construction.

The Prometheus fleet/archipelago, stationed off the coasts of Nigeria and Benin:

Al-Zarnuji: School and residential ship, with only a skeleton crew until the *Mount Parnassus* is well populated.

Archimedes: Manufacturing ship

Mount Parnassus: School and residential ship, the flagship.

CAST OF CHARACTERS

Aar Singh: BrainTrust Sikh peacekeeper.

Abshir: Somali twenty-something, cousin of Diric.

Ainsworth: Fleet Captain Jack Ainsworth, commander of the Fuxing fleet.

Alex Turner: Chief engineer of the *Argus*.

Alexei: Bodyguard for Dmitri, takes orders directly from the Premier of the Russian Union.

Amanda Copeland: Director of the *Chiron*'s medical department, current Chairman of the Board for the BrainTrust Consortium, Dash's supervisor.

Ben Wilson: Aging venture capitalist

Chance Dixon: Intern for Dash, Doctor of Medicine.

Chen Ying: Son of the Chinese Politburo, student on the *Taixue*.

Ciara Thornhill: Mission Commander for the Prometheus fleet, daughter of Lenora.

Colin Wheeler: BrainTrust resident

Dash: Dr. Dyah Ambarawati, medical researcher, polymath

Dawn Rainer: New head of the Rainer social media conglomerate. Daughter of Anne Rainer, who died undergoing rejuvenation therapy.

Dennis Gordon: Independent trucker specializing in delivering goods to California from out of state.

Diric: Somali teenager, pirate, student on the *Mount Parnassus*, cousin of Abshir.

Dmitri Mikhailov: Russian oligarch residing on the *Haven*.

Liu Fan Hui: Daughter of the Chinese Politburo, student on the *Taixue*.

Gao: Chinese Air Force Captain and squadron commander.

Gary Schott: Employee of SpaceR at the Hawthorne rocket factory.

Gina Toscano: Wife of Matt Toscano, Vogue model.

Gleb: Bodyguard for Dmitri.

Guang Jian: Son of the third member of the Chinese Standing Committee, student on the *Taixue*

Han Chunlan: Captain of the Chinese cruiser *Renhai* stationed near the Fuxing.

Hart Baddeley: Security Chief for the Fuxing

Jam: Pakistani commando, peacekeeper on the BrainTrust, Expedition Commander for the Fuxing fleet.

James Caplan, Ph.D.: Co-Founder of Accel, expert in scenario testing, one of the first pioneers to apply advanced technology to identification of people with leadership skills.

Joshua Pickett: BrainTrust mediator, stationed on the *Chiron* and then the *Haven*.

Julissa: Hukou peasant girl, student with the *Taixue*, serving as interpreter and guide for Jam in China.

Jun Laquan: Hukou peasant boy, student on the *Taixue*, inventor of the scuba bot Jacques.

Keenan Stull: Goldman Sachs financier

Kuo Lim: Baotong villager, husband of Shu Shi, father of missing daughter Liling.

Lenora Thornhill: Mission Commander for the Fuxing fleet, co-founder of Accel, mother of Ciara.

Lindsey Postrel: Owner/editor of Cogent News.

Marcos Ford: Peacekeeper for the Prometheus Fleet.

Matthew Toscano: CEO of SpaceR, husband of Gina Toscano.

Nuan: Elder and unofficial leader of the village of Baotong.

Ping: Peacekeeper for the BrainTrust, Security Chief for the Prometheus fleet.

Putu Arnawa: Peacekeeper for the Prometheus fleet.

Qi Ru: Hukou peasant, escaped China to attend Oxford, venture financing broker for the Fuxing.

Rhett Woodson: Nuclear engineer and designer for the primary isle ship reactors.

Shu Shi: Baotong villager, wife of Kuo Lim, mother of missing daughter Liling.

Song: Brilliant older hukou peasant from the Loess Plateau, father of Tai.

Suparman Herianto: aka Soup, peacekeeper for the Prometheus fleet.

Tai: Son of Song, hukou peasant diagnosed with web addiction.

Ted Simpson: Teenage developer of advanced homebrew copters.

Toni Shatski: Israeli Air Force Captain, engineering student at BTU.

Vasily: Bodyguard for Dmitri, takes orders directly from the Russian Union Premier.

Werner Halstead: Chief Engineer for SpaceR

Wolf Griffin: BrainTrust peacekeeper.

Xiu Bao: Hukou peasant girl, student on the *Taixue*.

Yefim: Bodyguard for Dmitri.

Zhang: Chinese Army Major commanding troops near the Loess Plateau.

1

WHEN LAST SEEN OUR HEROINES WERE...

True and unpopular ideas are what drive the world forward.
  —Sam Altman

Dash knocked politely on the open door of Chance's office. She had been there only a few times before. Normally the two of them spread their data out on a table in a conference room or huddled over a bank of computer screens in the lab compartment where they programmed the CRISPIER.

Before, the collage of pictures on the walls relentlessly displaying tattooed body parts had made Dash uncomfortable enough to keep her from seeing much. Today, because of Dash's increased awareness of hand-to-hand combat after the battle on Dmitri's yacht, one photo leapt out at her.

Two women faced off in a mixed martial arts ring. The woman delivering a ferocious kick to her opponent's head had her back to the photographer. Looking at the tattoos on the woman's arms and legs, however, Dash could now see clearly that the woman was Chance. The evidence of Chance's fighting skills, so surprising yet critical during the Russian Union Premier's attempt to kidnap her, had always been there for the seeing.

Chance waved her to a chair. "If our therapy continues to produce results like this it could get boring around here." Their latest batch of patients were all experiencing some level of successful rejuvenation.

Dash shook her head. "It cannot remain boring for long. We still have to figure out how to correct the therapy so it works for everyone." She pursed her lips. "I have been doing some preparatory work towards this, and I believe it is just about time to go back to it."

A look of horror crossed Chance's face and she shuddered. "Yeah, this has been nice, but we've been kind of avoiding the real work."

"Indeed. This has been a nice break, but it is time for us to return to battle." Dash pulled forth her tablet. "I have some ideas for some treatments we might be able to combine with basic telomere reconstruction. Some of these might reduce the risk while the telomere reconstruction was underway, while others may be able to increase the number of years a rejuvenation regains." Dash looked at the expression of dismay on Chance's face. She had clasped her hands together so tightly that Dash feared the nails would dig into the backs of her hands and draw blood.

Chance had clearly not quite steeled herself for the next round of experiments and the patient deaths that would consequently follow. Dash decided to give her a little time to prepare. "But we can do this tomorrow. Perhaps, for now, we should select another batch of easy patients."

Chance relaxed and drew out her own tablet. With a flick of her wrist, she passed a list of ten candidates over to Dash's tablet for consideration.

Dash perused the list. "I take it you ran these names past Dark Alpha 42?"

Chance shook her head. "Didn't need to. I picked them myself."

Dash laughed in surprise. "So you can follow Dark Alpha's algorithm now as well?" Dash had just recently trained herself to follow the algorithm, even though she still didn't understand it in any way she could express.

Chance shrugged. "Pretty much." A twinkle appeared in her eye. "You know, I tried feeding all the data from Dark Alpha into several of the AI systems that *can* explain their results."

Dash nodded. "As did I. I am pleased you did as well." It had been a test, sort of. Dash had wanted to see if Chance would take the initiative to find a better alternative for such an important problem. "Did you find anything?"

Chance sighed. "I found a couple that did better than you had done for your first set of test subjects, but none of them worked as well as Dark Alpha 42." She took another deep breath. "So I figured it would be best if I learned how to do it myself." The twinkle returned to her eye. "Now I'm just like you."

"So tell me. Explain the algorithm that discriminates between those who will receive rejuvenation and those who will die."

Chance snorted. "I can't explain it any better than you can. Apparently, I am now as nonhuman as you are."

"Aha. It is not really nonhuman, you know. There is a name for people like us who know the answer but can't explain it."

Chance raised her eyebrow.

"We are called 'experts.'"

Chance frowned. "Still, I think we'd be better experts if we could explain what our expertise tells us."

Dash shook her head. "No, Chance. There is another word in English for people who are not only expert but who can also explain what they know. Their title is more prestigious, but oddly, they often receive less respect."

Chance considered this for a moment, then gave up. "Okay, tell me. What is an expert who can explain himself called?"

Dash smiled. A faraway look entered her eyes. "Such a person is called a teacher."

Red Princeling Guang Jian knew everyone in the whole Fuxing/Prometheus merged archipelago watched him like hawks circling a squirrel. The way they all looked at him with so much distrust and loathing was comical. As if he could possibly care what these foolish Westerners thought.

Or foolish Politburo geeks for that matter. What had he ever done to Chen Ying to gain such obvious disrespect? Guang couldn't do much about the Westerners, but he knew that some time along the way he would have to teach Chen Ying some manners. Sure, Chen Ying was a son of the Politburo, but even Politburo members needed to show respect for the Standing Committee.

Right now, however, Guang was focused on getting more than just respect from Xiu Bao. He'd had his eye on the girl ever since coming aboard. At least she did not look at him with loathing. Actually, she didn't look at him at all, casting her eyes down any time he entered a room to find her. Generally, she then exited the room before he could even catch up to her to say something. But despite her avoidance and her shyness, he was confident she knew how to do her duty for a future member of the Standing Committee.

Which was what had brought him here to slouch against a passageway wall adorned with the images of tall skinny trees on the Sea of Bamboo Park deck on the *Taixue*. He had to admit the rendition of the park was not bad. He had been to the actual park, an hour or so outside Shanghai, several times. He'd even been on the cable car to the top of the mountain. He could see the rendering far down the passage, and it was an excellent reproduction of the real thing. People said the walk to the top of the mountain was delightful. Maybe so, but such journeys required far too much exertion for his taste.

The soft sound of footsteps on the passageway's deck caused him to look up. Sure enough, there was Xiu Bao shuffling with surprising speed toward her cabin, unaware of him lurking in the side passage. Guang licked his lips. Yes, he needed far more than just respect after such a long dry spell.

As Xiu Bao stepped into her cabin, Guang rushed across the passage and pushed the door back with one hand while pushing Xiu with the other. Another quick flick of the wrist and he drove the door shut behind him. She started to scream; he smacked her, mostly for the sheer pleasure of lashing out. No one yet lived in the adjacent cabins and there were no passersby, so he had not the least worry that someone might hear her. He let her scream again and smacked her once more.

Guang was correct that no humans had heard her scream, but they were not the only listeners aboard the ship. Had he, upon arrival aboard the *Taixue*, bothered to investigate the introductory module about isle ship features, he would have learned that the default settings for the vidcams in private cabins allowed the ship's AI to watch but not record. The AI looked only for indications of a terrible mishap—slipping in the shower and knocking yourself out, for example.

Guang's inattention to such detail was not matched by the AI. Xiu Bao had not modified the default settings, and the ship's AI heard her scream. It witnessed Guang's assault and followed its algorithms.

Ping spent much of her time on the *Taixue* for the simple reason that it was the only ship in the current merger of archipelagos that had a reasonable number of people on board. Well, the *Archimedes*, the manufacturing ship of her Prometheus fleet, had a fair number of people, all laboring furiously to complete the *Zhaozhou* manufacturing ship for the Fuxing fleet.

But the slow trickle of BrainTrust candidates and new members funneled onto the *Taixue*. Aside from the *Archimedes*, the rest of the ships had only skeleton crews aboard.

So Ping spent several hours every day training with her peacekeeping team on the empty *Mount Parnassus*, but then came over to the *Taixue* for lunch. This gave her the chance to hang out with Ciara, who was in turn hanging out with her mother Lenora as they worked with the new arrivals. There were certainly a satisfying number of amusing moments working with Ciara, but Ping was glad the *Zhaozhou* was ahead of schedule and the Prometheus fleet could soon depart for its new horizons.

Of course, Ping still had one piece of unfinished business she hoped to accomplish before they departed. When Jam had left for the Chinese mainland she had made Ping promise to watch for trouble among the newcomers, most notably from one particular Red Princeling. As if any promise were needed on that point!

So Ping was licking the remnants of lemon raspberry gelato from her ice cream cone when her earbud, along with the earbuds of all the other peacekeepers on the ship, sounded the alarm.

At last, some action! And very close at hand. Xiu Bao's cabin was one deck away, an easy run up the ramp. Not entirely by coincidence, of course. Ping, along with half the other peacekeepers, had been watching Guang play cat and mouse with the humble peasant girl for weeks. Ping's unfinished business looked to have come to fruition at last.

She flew up the ramp and flung herself headlong at Xiu's cabin door, which yielded to her security badge with a brief click. Once inside, Ping forced herself to take a moment to orient and ascertain what was happening.

Xiu lay dazed on her bunk, her eyes unable to focus although she turned her head in Ping's direction. She whispered something unintelligible. Guang had his pants unbuckled as he knelt between her legs. Seeing Ping, he stood up and turned to confront her.

Enough orientation. Ping charged at Guang screaming, a very different style of scream from what Xiu Bao had uttered earlier. Ping brought her knee up, targeting his tenderest parts, but too much adrenaline caused her to jump with excessive energy as Guang instinctively bent over to protect himself. He crouched too low; she kicked too high; Ping's knee cracked into the bottom of his rib cage.

As Guang's face twisted with pain, Ping slammed him against a bare wall. Xiu had arrived with pretty much nothing except the clothes on her back, and the room made Ping think of what Jam's room would have looked like when she had first arrived on the BrainTrust, with not a single ornament or weapon display in her possession, had she not had Ping to decorate the place.

After Guang thudded against the wall, Ping swung to break his nose—but Guang swiveled, and once again her timing was off. She struck him in the eye, bouncing his head off the wall. "Ow," she said, her knuckles having taken considerable damage from Guang's cheekbone.

Guang seemed to look at her with amazement, but it

was merely a vacant stare that happened to face in her direction. Guang, quite unconscious, slid to the floor.

"Damnation," Ping muttered with a frown. Although her hands were positioned to deliver a series of exquisite blows, she paused to watch him fall. With a sigh, she let her arms fall to her sides.

Security Chief Hart had arrived moments behind her. "What's wrong?" he asked in puzzlement. "You took him out with one blow. Pretty good, in my estimation."

"Exactly the problem, Chief," Ping continued mournfully. "It should have lasted longer. My focus failed, and with it my discipline." She looked up at the chief with concern. "Could I be losing my touch?"

Hart patted her on the shoulder. "Don't worry about it. We can spar tomorrow. Work out your frustrations on me." He smiled kindly. "While I'm wearing a thickly padded vest, of course."

Lenora, Hart, and Ping stood around Xiu Bao's hospital bed. Lenora held Xiu's hand. Both Ping and Hart unconsciously clenched and unclenched their fists.

Lenora spoke softly. "I am so sorry, Xiu. I was warned not to matriculate Guang in the first place, but I didn't listen."

Xiu smiled, a lopsided horror because the swollen half of her face stayed frozen. "The doctor tells me I'll be fine. I understand how hard it is to say no to our princelings."

Hart spoke. "We'll set up a mediation right away. He'll

pay you compensation till his ears bleed SmartCoins. His father will be furious with him."

Xiu jerked halfway out of her bed at this, but Ping was already raising her fist in the air. "Yes! We'll get Joshua to mediate by teleconference. He loves these kinds of cases." Her enthusiasm softened as she felt obligated to offer something closer to the truth. "Sort of."

Xiu's eyes glistened with tears. "Oh, no, please. You cannot do that."

Lenora squeezed her hand. "Xiu, our mediation system is not corrupt. You'll get a fair judgment."

Xiu shook her head. "It's not that. If you punish him, he'll take it out on my parents. He'll have them sent to a re-education camp." Her eyes bulged. "Or have them tried for treason."

Lenora recovered first. "I'll call them and bring them here to the Fuxing. Heaven knows, we have plenty of room."

"Thank you, but I don't think you'll be able to persuade them over the phone. They love their land and their friends and their lives." Xiu winced. "I'll have to go get them."

Lenora shook her head. "You aren't going anywhere, young lady."

Ping offered the obvious solution. "Jam's already dirt-side. She can be pretty persuasive."

Hart smiled. "That should work."

Lenora nodded. "In the meantime, I'll figure out how to break the news to Guang that he's done here." She smiled coldly. "I have an idea who might be pretty persuasive with him as well."

Jam looked out the window of the Range Rover at the Cradle of Chinese Civilization. Demonstrating once again her relentless strength of character, Jam neither curled her lip in disgust nor wept in despair. Her mission, to find the best and the brightest of Chinese peasants and bring them to the BrainTrust, had brought her here precisely *because* it was such an impoverished place. And yet, the area never should have been reduced to this.

Here in northern China, millennia earlier, the Qin dynasty had arisen. Qin Shi Huang had introduced a uniform currency, which had driven an immense surge in trade and wealth throughout the region. He had standardized the written language, allowing easy communication among all members of the empire. And he had gone so far as to allow peasants to own land, a radical innovation at the time.

It did not last. Dynasties rose and fell, while the lands that had cradled civilization fell and fell. And fell.

The nutritious topsoil so necessary for agriculture was, throughout the area, so loose that the plateau had eventually been named for it—the Loess Plateau. Any serious rain washed the topsoil away, down into the basins of the North China plain, where farmers farther to the east used the bounty to grow lush crops. Efforts had been made before and after the beginning of the twenty-first century to implement conservation policies to keep this land and its inhabitants productive.

But a perfect storm of woes had descended upon the land. Desertification swept in from the west. The conservation efforts provided mixed results. And worst of all, the farmers of the North China plain started to notice that the annual delivery of topsoil gifted to them from the plateau was decreasing. Being both richer and far better politically connected, the farmers of the North China plain had urged the government to constrain the conservation efforts on the plateau.

In Beijing political expediency intertwined with climatological reality in wondrous accord. Political support, educational efforts, and money for saving the plateau vanished along with the rain. Poverty and despair swept the land in tandem with the dust from relentless windstorms.

Looking on the bright side, the lands they had passed through for the last several days afforded, on a clear day, a kind of austere beauty that reminded Jam of her home a lifetime ago in Waziristan, although substantial differences remained. The most striking was probably the numerous terraced hillsides. The lessons of conservation had not been entirely lost.

Fortunately for travelers tired of staring at the parched landscape, Jam and her translator/native-guide/BrainTrust college student Julissa were descending into a half-hidden valley. The vegetation grew greener as they descended. When they reached the bottom, they found themselves passing—of all things—a long series of rice paddies.

A small group of men in the traditional short pants of rice farmers sat beneath an awning laughing. Periodically they pointed at an elderly gentleman standing out in the field, mud up to his calves, intensely working a pair of joysticks on a handheld box. A machine that Jam supposed to be some sort of rice paddy tiller coughed and hiccupped across the field, apparently controlled by the joysticks. The man, the tiller, and the joysticks all looked like they had come out of different centuries.

Julissa interrupted Jam's assessment. "We should find the fellow who got the exceptional Accel testing score in the village about a kilometer from here." The Accel testing app was the reason Jam and Julissa were out here in the middle of nowhere. Anyone with a cell phone could take the test to get a preliminary read on whether they qualified to become members of the BrainTrust. Those who could not make the trip to the Fuxing archipelago could wait and hope that Jam's traveling salesman algorithm would bring her to them.

Jam continued to watch the man in the field. "Stop the car."

"What?" Julissa asked even as she brought the car to the side of the road.

"This may only take a moment." Jam stepped from the car. "Or maybe a little longer."

Jam trudged out into the field, clutching her cell phone. The men under the awning stopped laughing and gaped at her. The old man with the joysticks, apparently disturbed by the sudden absence of people jeering at him, turned and watched as she approached. The tiller sputtered to a stop.

Jam forced a bright smile on her face as the mud soaked into her pants and squelched in her shoes. She had to laugh at herself. How easy it had been to adjust to the clean comfort of the BrainTrust. How difficult it was to accept this miserable mud. But she had been far more uncomfortable and miserable at times in the past. She endured.

And she offered a chipper greeting to the old gentleman. She hoped the chipperness made it through the translator app. "Good morning." She pointed at the joysticks, then at the tiller. "It looks like you're building a mighty fine robot there."

The farmer smiled. "The mayor's son broke his toy copter drone and I rescued it from the dumpster, thinking I might be able to use its parts to control my machine." He shrugged. "It's not yet clear if I will succeed, but I had to try. It would be so nice to sit on the side and let the tiller do the work without me."

Jam held up her cell phone, displaying the screening app. "Your bot here might be helping you in ways you could not anticipate. Could you go through this app and answer a few questions? It'll take about fifteen minutes, and I think it will be worth your time."

Twelve minutes later he handed the phone back. She studied the results; he more than qualified. "This is your lucky day. My name is Jam, by the way."

He looked at her in puzzlement. "Are you here to lift up the poor?"

Julissa had explained this phrase to her, the usual rhetoric used by Chinese bureaucrats in poor farmlands, where the residents understood that in the government lexicon, being poor also meant being backward, of low quality, and uncivilized. The implication was that the government would bring them into civilization...just as long as they remembered their place in the hukou system and continued as backward, low-quality peasant farmers.

Jam shook her head. She knew that people like Colin and Lenora had grand schemes to lift the poor far beyond any autocratic government's worst nightmares, but here today Jam had her feet firmly planted in the mud. "I am not here to lift the poor. I am here to lift *you*." She poked a finger ever so gently into his chest. "How would you like to come to the BrainTrust? Build real bots with real tools, new kinds of bots that have never been seen before."

"I'd like nothing better." His eyes shone. "My name is… " He paused, clearly thinking about the name Jam had offered. "Call me Song."

"Song. Good to meet you."

Song's smile faded as he thought about his situation. "Alas, I cannot come to the BrainTrust. My son is in the addict's re-education center. I cannot leave him."

Jam shook her head in astonishment. "An addict?" She looked at the dirt roads and the tall barren mountains. "They have drugs like heroin and cocaine here?"

Song shook his head. "No, no. He is a computer addict. He spends over six hours a day on the web."

Jam had heard that, in China, the local mythology held that six hours was the most a person could spend on a computer without suffering an addiction with serious side effects. She had thought it was a joke. She tried to imagine Dash restricted to six hours online per day. In less than a week, Dash would be pulling out her hair and screaming for mercy. Jam had to keep herself from laughing at the vision. "Take me to see your son," she demanded. Rehabilitation indeed! For people who spend too much time exploring the rest of the world, comparing it to the lives they have no hope of changing! Jam would show them rehabilitation, all right.

On board the *Chiron*, the clocks had just struck midnight. The hallway and the lab were dark, yet light glowed from the conference room.

Dash stared at a new list of patients. Chance stared at Dash. Silence reigned.

In the recent runs of Dash's rejuvenation therapy, no one had died. Candidates who would have died had been refused admission to the process.

Moving on, to try to save the rejected patients would mean more deaths by therapy. Dash had finally been pushed to step up to the challenge when one candidate had died the day after being rejected. Dash might refuse to take risks with patients, but Nature had no such qualms.

The search for solutions had become so desperate that Dash had resorted to old school methods, conducting experiments with mice until she had something that seemed likely to work...about half the time. "So," she said as much to herself as to Chance, "if things go as we hope, in this next batch of ten patients five will rejuvenate to some extent, one will experience no change, and the other four will die."

Chance tried to cheer her up. "Just remember, they all had one foot in the grave already." Trying to distract her, Chance changed topics. "What was that last criterion you used to get down to just ten patients, anyway?"

When Dash responded, it was clear that this was not as great a change of topic as Chance had hoped. "That was the Dark Alpha forecast for how long the candidates would live without therapy. Every one of the patients we will now experiment upon has less than three months to live."

Chance raised an eyebrow. "Dark Alpha can predict that?"

"It doesn't even require Dark Alpha to make these forecasts. They had an AI in 2018 that could make these predictions rather reliably, but the tech more or less died out."

Chance thought she knew why. "Let me guess. Regulatory interference?"

"Not at all. It died because no one wanted to use it. The doctors all thought that if their patients learned they had only months to live it would make them despondent, driving a self-fulfilling prophecy." Dash gave Chance a wry smile. "I didn't use it myself for the same reason."

Chance guessed the next step. "But now you'll use it because you have a better offer to make to the patients. They can die in three months, or they can roll the dice."

Dash nodded. "Exactly."

They finally closed up shop. As they walked back to their adjacent cabins, Dash found her thoughts wandering to her friends, Ping and Jam. She hoped Jam's new job as dirtside Expedition Commander was turning out well, and she hoped Ping had found some action. But there were hardly any people in the new archipelagos just yet. It seemed unlikely that Ping could have found any worthy mayhem in which to indulge. Poor Ping, with nothing to do.

2

IN DEEP

Write an addictive app using at least five of the gratification-inducing techniques discussed earlier. The top three apps will be presented to Wilson Ventures for startup funding consideration.

—Accel. Topic: Mind Manipulation. Module: User Interface Final Project.

Fortress, prison, boot camp. The web-addiction rehabilitation facility looked like all three rolled into one. Well, on the bright side, at least the guards weren't carrying machine guns. The concertina wire along the tops of the walls did not look inviting, however.

Jam could hear a drill sergeant's voice booming from the inside yard as she and Song entered the reception area. Visits by parents were encouraged, Song told her, as long as they weren't too often or too long. Bad for discipline, he explained with a sanguine acceptance of the claims of the experts.

Song's son Tai came in, wearing a gray uniform far too big around the waist but clearly too tight in the shoulders. It made her old burkas look stylish and form-fitting.

Another man, taller, with a round face, came in with him. "Good afternoon, Song. As you can see, Tai is doing just fine."

Song introduced them. "Headmaster, this is… Jam." He looked at his son. "She wants me to go with her to the BrainTrust."

Tai's eyes lit up. "That's awesome, Dad." He looked away and stuttered, "I'll be okay here."

Tai was thinner than his father, but he did not look unhealthy. Indeed, you could just begin to see the development of some much-needed muscle across his chest.

However ridiculous the concept of web addiction might be, Jam thought the experience of being here had not been entirely a waste for Song's son. Jam reached into her pocket. "I'm hoping you can go with him. I have a little test I'd like you to take, to see what kinds of talents you have." She pulled out her tablet.

The headmaster barked, "Stop!"

Jam froze in astonishment. "What?"

The headmaster sneered. "Electronic devices are strictly forbidden here." He drew himself to his full height and glowered at Jam as if he were her commanding officer. "If you cannot be civilized, you'll have to leave."

Jam had noticed that the headmaster had gotten angry the moment Song suggested that Tai might be leaving. The headmaster could have been either a very caring man or a very greedy one who hated letting his profits go. Jam didn't care.

The secret truth was that, even if Tai did poorly on the test, she was going to accept him onto the BrainTrust. Bringing family members was a routine part of onboarding new members. Jam had mostly been curious whether, as she suspected, web addiction might be caused in the imaginative mind—a BrainTrust quality mind—by desperation. In retrospect, Jam realized she probably should have saved the testing till they had gotten him out of this place.

But the headmaster's next words suggested it would not have made any difference. "Your son can't leave at this time, Song. He's in a delicate state."

Jam raised her eyebrows. Tai didn't look at all delicate to her. Thin, yes, but he had a steady gaze. He reminded her a little bit of Ping. It made her want to rescue him even more. When she realized that she was thinking of it explicitly in terms of a rescue operation, her determination hardened.

The headmaster continued to speak. "Even if I would consider releasing him, which I will not, you've paid to the end of the semester. Don't expect a refund."

Song looked back and forth between the headmaster and Jam nervously. "I don't care about the money if it's really okay for him to go with me." He looked at his son. "How are you feeling, Tai? Would it hurt you to take this little test? It's short, I promise. Jam already gave it to me."

Before Tai could answer, the headmaster reiterated his stance. "No! Absolutely not."

Jam pursed her lips. Such a tiresome fellow. She glided around the table to stand next to the headmaster, very close. She reached out and took his hand. Then shifting her body to obscure her actions she twisted his hand in a thumb lock. She whispered, "Let me give him this test, and let him go, or you will be explaining at the nearest hospital how the little foreign girl accidentally broke your thumb."

The headmaster did not wince though Jam knew the pain was considerable. His eyes bulged ever so slightly, however, in testament to silent suffering. The two of them stood in tableau for a moment; in the end he relented. "Go ahead."

Jam squeezed his shoulder as if he were her new best friend, and smiled. "Thank you." She returned to Tai and handed him the tablet. She gave him the same truncated version of the test she had given Song in the rice paddy; ten minutes later it was over. Jam smiled as she looked at the results. Tai might not be quite as brilliant as his dad, but he would have made a fine addition to the community even without his father. "Excellent. If you want to come with us, you're more than welcome."

Tai smiled, but a worried look clung to him. "What about my addiction?"

The headmaster opened his mouth to speak; Jam glared; he stayed silent.

Jam answered. "I think you'll find that on the Brain-Trust these addictions rapidly pass away." She decided it would be too much information if she told him that in the near future he would probably be spending twelve hours a day, not six, hunched over his computer. Fortunately, Accel forced the students to take breaks, get some exercise, and socialize. And if Jam had anything to say about it, Tai would continue the serious physical training he'd been getting in rehab. She suspected it had done him some good, however ridiculous the local beliefs that put him here. Something to remember to mention to Lenora.

She looked back at Song. "Let's go."

As they walked through the gate to their car, Jam breathed the free air gratefully. Time to pursue her other thought. "Tai, do you think any of the other kids in rehab here have the qualifications to join the BrainTrust?"

Tai pondered for a moment. "I think so." He shrugged. "I'd like to test them first."

Song offered, "I know at least some of the parents. Understand, this rehabilitation center draws people from all over the province."

Jam halted for a moment as a blaze of insight blinded her. She remembered her last conversation with Lenora: *"Really, Lenora? You want to send me into the middle of a million square miles of desolation to look personally for applicants? You already made the app available to everyone with a cell phone so they could test themselves. Why not just let them prove their grit by making their way out here on their own?"*

Lenora had looked down her nose at her. *"We have no way of knowing what forces can prevent the app from being available, or being used, or being believed. We have little understanding of the obstacles they will face making the journey, though we do know that those obstacles will vary wildly from person to person. It's true you're searching for candidates, and doing validation of the results for people who passed the test on their own. And you'll fund their journey to get here because it may take a lot more grit to get here than is appropriate for the testing. But those are only the visible parts of your mission. What you're really looking for is the information that will make our quest a success. Improve the app, improve the process. We face too many unknown unknowns for my taste. I'm counting on you to make the unknowns known."*

These rehabilitation centers represented just the sort of unknowns Lenora sought. The kids inside couldn't take the test, even though these "web addicts" might be a lot more likely than the general populace to qualify as Brain-Trust material. She realized that, all unwittingly, people like the headmaster were concentrating some of the best and brightest into high-density targets for Lenora's project. Jam could just imagine Lenora doing quick sharp raids on all these "rehabilitation" centers, recruiting the community for her archipelago far faster than expected.

Jam smiled. "Well, let's see how many parents we can find, and how many of the prisoners we can help escape."

Tai objected. "It's not a prison. It's just a place to help people overcome their problems."

Jam decided not to argue. "Of course. We'll assess how many ...addicts... are qualified for the BrainTrust. We'll go from there."

Jun Laquan had always dreamed of the sea. He did not know why. He did not question it. He'd never seen the sea before his parents brought him here to the Fuxing archipelago.

But he had read about the sea on the web for years. In the evening, after washing the dishes, he would study pictures and videos of scuba divers. They looked so free.

Then he would get up in the morning and help his parents work in the fields of hard red winter wheat, or clean the latrine next to the dirt road, hoping to find that a passerby had peed or pooped, leaving human waste that would serve in the fields as valuable fertilizer. Dreaming as he did so of the sea.

So when he arrived on the Fuxing, the first thing he did was learn to swim. Other new arrivals, his parents included, took the mandatory swimming instruction with reluctance and grumbling. But he jumped into the pool and laughed and spun in the water and soon qualified to teach the swimming classes.

Next, he'd learned to snorkel, and plunged into the water in the protected patch of water formed within the rectangle of anchored isle ships. Of course, there was little to see in this water, but he dived as deep as he could. The diver's watch Ms. Lenora had given him showed he'd reached ten meters, a nice depth for his next adventure, since he planned to learn to scuba dive.

And here his driving ambition had met the immovable object of adult supervision. "Jun," Lenora explained gently, "you're too young to be scuba diving just yet. Your lungs— your whole body— is still maturing, still forming. We can't let you be subjected to the high-pressure forces of scuba for a couple years. Wait till you're sixteen. The ocean will still be there."

Well, there was more than one way to dive into the ocean.

Jam's next hurdle arrived with dinner in the town's wooden shack of a restaurant. As she picked up a steaming bun molded in the shape of a piglet, Jam explained her plan for Song and Tai. First, she handed Song a debit card. "I want the two of you to get to the Fuxing archipelago ASAP. Your first job will be to help Lenora Thornhill, our Mission Commander, put together a strategy for testing candidate members who have been swept up into web addiction rehabilitation centers."

She paused for a moment to chew a mouthful of bun. "In the morning, we'll drive you to the nearest train station, which can take you to an airport, to get you to Shanghai or Hong Kong." She handed a spare cell phone to Tai. "Use this phone to contact the BrainTrust. Lenora's phone number is on speed dial; she'll direct you to whoever is going to handle the last part of your journey—getting you onto a ferry out to the archipelago."

Jam leaned forward to emphasize her next point. "Use this phone only. Your own phones may be blocked at any time for various reasons." Particularly if the headmaster wanted to make a stink, Jam thought. There were no back doors on her phone to allow the Chinese government or friends of government to eavesdrop, and though they could follow the message traffic, they had no way of knowing this phone belonged to Tai now. The ubiquitous surveillance in China could still find them, but it would take a little more juice and better political connections.

Song was shaking his head. "I can't take the train. Or any airplane in China."

Jam stared at him for a moment.

Julissa recognized the problem. "I see. 'Once untrustworthy, always restricted,' correct?" When Song nodded, Julissa turned to Jam. "Song here has bad social credit according to the government's calculations." She turned back to Song. "What did you do?"

Song looked away sheepishly. "When I was nineteen, I joined a protest against the provincial governor's plan to take half our village's land for a factory." He shrugged. "We would've been happy enough to sell him the land, but to just *take* it? Anyway, everybody in the protest got permanent social credit downgrades."

Jam rolled her eyes. Then the phone in her pocket rang. She recognized the ring, *School's out for Summer.* "Lenora, how can I help you?" Jam listened as Lenora explained about Guang's attempted rape. A smile tugged at Jam's lips as she visualized Ping bursting into the cabin, giving him the opportunity to experience an assault firsthand from the victim's point of view. She couldn't resist asking, "Is Guang in the brig or the hospital?"

Lenora hesitated. "He'll be in the brig shortly. His injuries turned out to be not as severe as they seemed at first."

So, hold on a moment. Ping restrained herself? Against a rapist? Jam would have to call the girl to find out what really happened.

Her pleasure at the thought of talking with Ping faded as Lenora explained what she wanted Jam to do. Jam tried to object. "You want me to go where? You want me to do what?" Jam pulled out her tablet and looked at the map. "Do you have any idea how far it is from here to get to Xiu Bao's parents?"

As Lenora argued in her methodical and relentless way for Jam to do as ordered, Jam realized there was an upside to this plan: it would get her as well as Song out of the area, far out of the area. The more she had reflected over the course of the afternoon on her encounter with the headmaster, the more she thought the headmaster might try to make things hot for her for a while. A short trip to a faraway place seemed a wise precaution. "Okay Lenora, you win. We'll leave first thing in the morning."

As Jam put the phone away, she explained to her companions about the princeling and the assault and the victim's fear for her parents. "New plan. We're all going to drive together into the Southwest. We'll find Xiu's parents, persuade them to join their daughter, and send all of you to Vietnam. You'll take this Range Rover. Somebody from the archipelago will take you from there."

Tai brought up the obvious problem. "What about you? You'll be stuck without your vehicle."

Jam frowned. "We can buy or rent another Rover." When she thought about the grueling journey through the Chinese backcountry, she felt exhausted. "Perhaps someone on the BrainTrust can think of something better."

<hr>

Oligarch Dmitri Mikhailov sat behind his luxurious desk in his luxurious mansion on the luxurious isle ship *Haven* and glared at his phone. He'd been putting off making this call ever since Mediator Joshua first requested it. *You'll make a profit on it,* Joshua had asserted. *Think of it as compensation for the victims,* he'd said, without ever mentioning which victims it was for. Dmitri had to confess, there were more than one.

The phone connected and started ringing. *Please, please*

go to voicemail, he thought.

"Professor Thornhill speaking," the crisp disembodied voice came back to him.

"Ah, this is Dmitri Mikhailov. Are you the Fuxing Mission Commander?"

"Mikhailov! About time you called. I was wondering if I was going to have to have Joshua kick you a couple of times."

Dmitri winced. "As you can see, no need." His lip curled into a snarl, but she could not see it. He dropped the expression and choked out the critical words. "How can I help you?"

Her laugh was dry, raspy. "I need an instructional module. You're the perfect person to write it for me." She explained about the Accel Educational Framework, and the independent authors who created all the modules. "So you see, you can work off your debt to Joshua by making a profit with me. Possibly a substantial profit."

Dmitri's own voice turned dry. "Substantial? Do you understand who I am?"

Thornhill coughed. "Right, a billionaire oligarch. Ok, forget that last. You can still make some nice pocket change. Or donate it for scholarships for those more deserving than you. Heaven knows we can use all the scholarships we can get our hands on for the students arriving here. Or better yet from your perspective might be student investments, upfront funding in return for a piece of any inventions they develop further down the line."

Dmitri had to admit, that almost sounded interesting. "I'll give it some thought. In the meantime, what is it I need to do? What instructional module do you want me of all people to write? I doubt it would be useful for your students to learn how to persuade the Premier of the Russian Union to give you monopoly rights on weapons exports."

"What I need is not unrelated to that. I need a module on ethics. Comparing and contrasting ethical uses of wealth and power to unethical uses."

Dmitri laughed explosively. "Me? Ethics?"

"I know of no one who has looked at ethics from so many different directions. Consider it: After becoming a henchman in supplying weapons to mass murderers, you attempted to kidnap an innocent young doctor, and then had to beg that doctor to save you from your other henchmen. Joshua claims you now act as if you were an ethical person with high moral standards." She paused. "Honestly, I'd be just as happy to see you tossed outside the reef as chum for the sharks, but the ethics of your victims pretty much removes that option from the table."

Dmitri thought Ping might be willing to do the deed. Hopefully, Ping and this professor would not share thoughts on the matter.

"Anyway, I can't imagine anyone as qualified as you to put together a richer, more thoughtful analysis of ethics and their practical application in the real world." Her voice turned ever so slightly ironic. "First, of course, you should read the existing ethics modules to see how they fall short. In addition to contributing to making the modules better, you might even learn something." She went back to emphasize an earlier point. "But it's that practical aspect of putting ethics to use in the real world that only you can present with unique insight. Teach the students how to avoid being like you."

The woman had an odd style of salesmanship. Of course, she could always ask Joshua to lean on him. Technically, Joshua had no power over him at this point. But the way things seemed to go around here, best not to get Joshua—or this professor—angry with him. "Writing these modules, am I going to have to do any programming?"

At this implicit acceptance of the job, the professor's voice turned cheery. "Not a problem. I'll have my associate Dr. Caplan, who was one of the inventors of the Accel platform, come over and help you with the mechanics."

Dmitri sighed. "I'll look into it."

"Excellent. And thank you, Mr. Mikhailov. I think you'll find it's fun, in the end."

Dmitri doubted that very much, but he'd see.

On the Chinese mainland people generally thought of Chen Ying first as a Red Princeling. Here on the Fuxing archipelago of the BrainTrust, he found it refreshing to be thought of first as an alpha geek.

He finished the module on linear differential equations and gave it a four-star rating. The module had been pretty easy to follow, given the complexity of the material. Still, he thought he could do better.

He was contemplating writing an alternative differential equation module and submitting it to Accel just to see what it was like to submit a module and to see if he could really do better. He thought it might be fun.

Which explained, he thought sourly, why he could never get a girlfriend. Being an alpha geek might be less stressful, but this was one of its drawbacks. He thought he could probably use his father's name to shock and awe one of the peasant girls into dating him, but that did not feel quite right.

A shadow fell across his right side, and he could just detect the hint of Professor Thornhill's perfume. He looked up questioningly.

"Congratulations," the professor told him. "You're now way ahead of the other students."

Chen Ying grimaced. "It's hardly impressive to be ahead of Guang. Has he completed even one module since he arrived?" Since he'd arrived on the Fuxing and had to team up with Guang Jian on a number of team projects, he'd developed a considerable dislike for the person who would, because of his father, be forever his superior.

Professor Thornhill chuckled. "He's actually done pretty well. We suspect Fan is doing over half the work for him and bribing or blackmailing him into doing the rest, but we're letting that go." Professor Thornhill's voice took on a lower, darker tone. "For the moment."

So, the professor didn't like Guang anymore than he did. But Guang was still getting away with it, just like always. Still, the professor's last words suggested that, just perhaps, this was going to be another Cambridge for the blasted jerk.

The professor moved on to the topic she wished to discuss. "It's time for you to have a new experience. I want you, as part of your education, to become a tutor." She shifted her head back and forth. "Really, you'll be acting like a full-fledged Accel professor, helping students with their hands-on projects." She paused. "One particular student, anyway."

Chen gave her a sideways smile. "So you're going to use me as free labor. Do I get a discount on my tuition?"

The professor just shook her head with a smile. "Not a chance. But you will get a very fine commendation in your school record."

Chen sighed. "Well, I guess that's something…" He slouched and stared at her. "So which student am I your slave for?"

Thornhill slid her finger across her tablet, tossing data on to Chen's machine. "Jun Laquan. He's one of our brightest." She hesitated. "He's on a par with you."

Chen sat up a little straighter, no longer slouching. "I'm one of your best, huh?"

The professor ignored this. "He's become fascinated with scuba diving. Since he's too young to scuba dive himself, I think he's trying to build a robot to go diving for him."

Chen raised an eyebrow. "Really? I suppose it wouldn't be too hard, with the underwater reef-maintenance bots to start with."

"Perhaps. Regardless, I want you to help him. And any other problems he has with his modules, you'll be his first line of help."

Chen rolled his eyes. "There's no way I can get out of this, can I?"

The professor beamed at him. "I knew you'd volunteer."

3

HITTING BOTTOM

Confirmation Bias: A well-known flaw of the human thinking apparatus is its willingness to accept, without critical thought, a claim that fits neatly with the mind's pre-existing belief system. Below is a short questionnaire to assess your belief system. Based on that profile, a readily absorbed claim will be presented. The student is required to dissect the claim and identify at least two reasons why it is wrong...

—Accel Topic: Critical Thinking. Module: Failure Modes

Jun Laquan marveled as he started tinkering with the robots made available to the older students for experiments. His new tutor, Chen Ying, seemed interested in helping and apparently stole them for him. Chen had held his finger to his lips in a shushing motion. "Don't tell anyone."

So with Chen's help, Jun took the body of the reef

tending bot and gave it the head from a butler bot. He attached the remote-controlled arms and hands from a remote-controlled nuclear reactor bot, incorporating its haptic feedback systems. Now he had a human-looking scuba-diving bot. The least humanoid part was the propulsion impellers where the legs should have been.

Very late one night, he and Chen Ying took the new bot, which they named Jacques, to the swimming pool on the Gilligan deck and threw it in. It sank swiftly to hit the bottom with a thud. Fortunately, no cracks in the concrete radiated from the point of impact.

Jun muttered, "Buoyancy compensators need reprogramming." He pulled on his gloves. "I can still test it, give it a little thrust to get off the bottom." He pushed his hands down and they saw the bot do a push-up, lifting off the bottom. Jun applied a little more power, and the bot started moving. "Yes!" Jun cried, then started the bot spinning in the water, a graceful movement. He used his right hand to sweep water underneath, reversing the spin. Jun's glove reached his chest at the end of the sweep.

The bot's hand continued to sweep, and its hand plunged into its chest where, on a human, the heart would have been.

Jacques did not, of course, have a heart, but the equipment buried in the left side of the chest was critical enough that it might as well have been a heart. The bot spun lazily as it crashed into the bottom. It sputtered and jerked as if being electrocuted, which, in a sense, was a correct interpretation.

Chen Ying sighed. "The limiter failed open."

Jun winced. "Limiters are supposed to be very reliable."

The limiter was the mechanism, attached to a movable part like a limb, that stopped the limb before it crashed into other parts of the bot. When a limiter "failed open" it stopped limiting.

Chen said gently. "They may not be as reliable if they get wet. Looks like the seal failed."

Jun shook his head. "It's going to be really hard to retrieve it now."

Chen frowned. "You need to add something that will automatically inflate the ballast tanks and bring it back to the surface if something goes wrong."

Jun Laquan nodded, then jumped into the pool to struggle with the bot to bring it back to the surface. Eventually, Chen brought in a cargo carrying bot and the three of them together were able to retrieve poor Jacques.

"Here are the keys, Mr. Toscano." Ted Simpson held out a pair of simple black dongles for him.

Matt Toscano, CEO of SpaceR, took the keys and looked at the latest, greatest copter brought forth from the creative genius of Ted Simpson. Sleek and graceful, the copter practically screamed its need for speed. "She's beautiful, Ted. You matched the colors perfectly." The red and gold paint job looked just like the suit of armor in the reception area of the SpaceR HQ on board the *Argus*, the manufacturing ship in the original BrainTrust archipelago that was still manufacturing rockets for SpaceR while SpaceR's *Helios* isle ship was still under construction.

"Thank you, Mr. Toscano." His enthusiasm rose. "But

even better, it has the extended range you asked for." He paused. "Though I'm not quite sure where you're planning to go."

Matt laughed. "I'm not sure where I'm going either, but now I'm more confident I'll be able to get there." That was not quite true. He had a specific goal in mind: he needed to be able to fly all the way from the BrainTrust to Reno, Nevada without stopping. The BrainTrust had no airport. The copters were the only way of flying in or out, and he was *persona non grata* throughout the Great State of California. Getting back and forth to SpaceR's launch facility in Boca Chica Texas currently required traveling by ferry to Mexico, then getting from Mexico into Texas through the customs bureaucrats at the border. Even with pale white skin and an American passport, the border checkpoint was a brutal lesson in regulatory stupidity.

Ted shifted uneasily. "If there's nothing else you need, I gotta go. I'm doing a rush job for Dr. Dash." His eyes gleamed. "I think you'll like the next generation copter. If you're still on the outs with the California government, it'll be useful to you."

Matt raised an eyebrow. "That sounds interesting. Though honestly, now that you've built this for me, I doubt the governor will be much of an issue."

Ted looked doubtful. He obviously knew all the different ways California had tried to hurt his number one investor. "Ok. See ya."

Ted started to walk away but stopped, half-bowing to someone coming toward Matt. "Mrs. Toscano! Good to see you."

Matt heard his wife's throaty laugh. "You too, Ted."

Once she was sure Ted was gone and Matt's eyes were locked on her, Gina started swaying her hips. She unbuttoned her coat, beneath which she wore only a metallic yellow bikini. "Hey, lover," she breathed.

Dropping the coat, she poured herself across the new copter. Her bikini matched the yellow paint accents of the vehicle.

As she slithered through a half-dozen positions, Matt murmured, "Never saw you pose like that while you were modeling for Vogue."

She slunk over to him. "Just for my husband."

Matt shook his head to clear his mind. He dangled his keys side to side as if trying to hypnotize her. "I figured I'd take the new copter for a test drive."

She whispered in his ear. "Thank you for inviting me." She scooped up her coat and wrapped it back around her.

As they departed the *Haven*, Matt headed into the Southwest.

Gina gurgled, "Field trip!"

Matt explained. "The new reef."

"Natch." She looked over her shoulder at the rapidly-dwindling cluster of isle ships. "Fast."

"Mine."

Gina pouted briefly, then pointed out the front toward a tiny white dot on the horizon.

Matt answered her question. "The methane tank where they store our fuel before offloading to the tankers."

As they approached, an ugly gray cylinder and a two-story building came into view, separated by a beach of hard-packed sand.

Finally, they could see an enormous ring, miles in

diameter, kelp green on each edge with a center band of dull black sheets.

Gina looked at the black sheets in surprise. "Solar panels? No nukes?"

"Surprised me too. Surely cost effective. The BrainTrust isn't religious about power generation."

Gina smiled. "Pure pragmatism."

"Thank heavens."

Matt dropped the copter down to the beach next to the two-story building. At the other end of the beach a soccer match of deadly earnestness, involving four children, progressed apace.

Matt considered landing in the water. Ted had assured him the copter floated quite reliably. But unlike Gina with her bikini, Matt was improperly dressed to go splashing in the water.

A middle-aged couple holding hands and wearing Hawaiian shirts approached them. The man spoke in heavily accented but understandable English. "Mr. Toscano? I'm Pedro, this is my wife Marta."

After a short round of introductions, Gina pointed at the soccer players. "You have beautiful children."

Marta beamed at her. "Thank you. They are hard to keep up with, but they are worth it."

Matt looked at them in puzzlement. "Dash told me you didn't speak a lick of English. I expected we'd have to run our whole conversation through our cell-phone translators. Your language skills are amazing."

Pedro laughed. "The kids have to learn English if they're going to go to the BrainTrust for college, so we have to learn it too." He pulled his cell phone out of his shirt pocket and tapped it. "Dr. Dash gave us the latest in educational programs. Accel."

Gina eyed the children thoughtfully. "BrainTrust University is awfully hard to get into."

Marta answered. "Very hard." She puffed up proudly. "But Accel says our eldest son is progressing fast enough, he may qualify."

Pedro added. "And with university extensions opening in both the Fuxing and Prometheus archipelagos, perhaps it will be easier for our younger ones." He pointed at the building nearest them. "Can we give you a tour?"

Matt rubbed his hands together. "By all means."

Pedro started to explain. "This is the building where the bots bring the algae for cooking." He pointed to a pipe running out of the building. "The methane comes out that pipe, to run into the storage tank further around the reef."

He pointed to a secondary pipe much smaller than the first, going to a small tank by the building. "One of the new things we've added is this secondary chemical converter that extracts oil and converts it to diesel. So we can refill your copter if you'd like before you depart."

Matt nodded. "Sounds like a plan."

The tour continued, though there was not much to see. Marta eventually interrupted. "Would you like a cup of tea?"

Gina gushed, "We'd be delighted. I confess I'd love to see your place." She pointed at the gray cylinder, which was attached to the outer rim of the reef. "I presume that's your house?"

Marta's face lit up. "Yes, it is." She looked away. "It's probably a bit small compared to what you're used to."

Pedro countered. "But it's really cozy. Marta has done a great job on it. It's not just a house," he said as if fumbling for words, "it's a home."

The wind picked up as they moved more briskly to the house. Matt looked around. Aside from the children, as far as the eye could see nothingness stared back, an endless expanse of emptiness save for the dark clouds now moving towards them at a visibly faster clip. "Storm coming," he observed.

Pedro eyed the wind whipped storm front. "You still have a little time."

As Marta opened the front door, she started the description. "We have four levels. Each is quite tiny, of course, but it's still a very nice space."

They entered to find a diminutive kitchen and dinette area. The built-in appliances, like the appliances on the BrainTrust, were top of the line, while the furniture looked rickety from years of exposure to sea mist.

As Marta turned to make the tea, Pedro pointed up the ladder to the next level. "Up there is our living room. All the windows give us a great view." He pointed down the ladder going below decks. "And that way we have two bedroom levels. The first one is for the kids, the bottom one is for us. It's a lot more privacy than we had in our place back home."

A higher pitched but still male voice, a teenager, piped up. "It's really six levels, but Mom and Dad always forget to mention the two bottom levels with the batteries." Unlike his parents, he spoke like a native of California.

"Shush," Marta said.

Pedro introduced them. "Mr. and Mrs. Toscano, let me

introduce our son Paolo. He wants to be a nuclear engineer." Pedro shook his head in bemusement. "Very different from his father."

It was Matt's turn to laugh. "They do that sometimes I'm told."

Gina looked at the boy appreciatively. "I was surprised to see solar panels covering the reef. I thought the BrainTrust was all about the nukes. I'd guess you'd be happier if you had a nuke here to study."

The boy bobbed his head eagerly. "Dr. Dash says the solar panels are the best answer for our needs. We run the processing plant and recharge the bots during the day. Then the bots do the harvesting and reef maintenance at night. We only need enough batteries to keep our home running for a couple of days when there's a bad storm."

Matt saw a problem. "In storms like that, with those winds, don't the solar panels blow away?"

Pedro shrugged. "They're cheap. We always lose a few in the worst storms. Dr. Dash says they figured that into the calculations, and we have spare panels in storage. After a storm, the bots go out and replace any that are damaged."

Paolo pursed his lips. "The big problem is that the batteries are so dangerous. Dr. Dash says it's ok, but we're living on a bomb."

Gina stared at him, baffled.

Matt laughed. "Batteries sometimes explode, you know." He shook his head. "Unlike the BrainTrust's nuclear power plants, as Dash explained to me once, ever so eloquently."

Paolo offered, with a teenager's excitement, "Would you like to see a video of batteries like ours exploding?"

Marta put teacups down around the table, banging them a little hard. "No! We don't need to watch any explosions."

Matt added, "Honestly, we've seen enough explosions lately."

Marta shushed Paolo out of the house. When she sat down, the battered old table rocked back and forth once on its uneven legs.

Marta apologized. "I'm sorry. We really should get a new table. But we're putting all our money into the college fund."

A wicked gleam entered Pedro's eye. "A fair part of it is invested in SpaceR stock."

Marta brought a bowl of fruit to the table. "Would you like an orange? We've started growing them here on the reef. It's about the only thing we have except for the shrimp and the sardines that grow along the edge of the reef."

Matt demurred, but Gina took one and stripped the skin. "Very fresh," she observed.

Matt looked out the windows at the endless horizon. "You know, there are days when I would find it very attractive to live here."

Gina shuddered. "But you'd live here without me."

Matt wrapped an arm around her. "And that's why it'll never happen."

Pedro smiled. "I know that it seems terribly isolated. But we're not, you know. We still have the Internet."

Matt, still looking out the windows, watched as dark clouds rolled in. "I'm looking at the storm heading this way, and I can't help worrying about how exposed you are out here. How much danger are you really in? Should we be evacuating you during these storms?"

Pedro shook his head. "When it gets really bad, we can pull our house away from the reef and submerge this level so that only the living room is at sea level. It's quite safe."

Marta felt obligated to defend their situation. "It's certainly safer than his old job."

Matt looked at him in surprise. "What was your old job?"

Marta answered. "He was a fisherman. We grew up in a small Peruvian fishing village."

Gina leaned forward. "So how did you get here?"

Pedro explained, "My brother and his family brought us in for an interview and gave us a recommendation. His family maintains the reef two hundred miles off the coast of San Francisco when the BrainTrust is anchored in the fifty-mile reef. And when the BrainTrust moves out to two hundred miles, he moves in to take care of the fifty-mile reef."

Matt realized this answered another question. "So, when all your children go to college, if you need help you can probably call in a cousin or two."

Marta nodded. "They would all jump at the chance to live in this isolated place. Just for the water, if nothing else."

Gina blinked. "The water?"

Marta continued. "We have all the fresh water we can drink. We don't have to worry about diseases and trash in the water. It's a godsend."

Such a simple thing that Matt and Gina had taken for granted their entire lives rendered them speechless.

Pedro glanced out the window and a worried look crossed his face. "The storm is approaching very fast. You two should go now."

Marta threw in an invitation. "You're welcome to stay, of course."

Pedro continued. "But you might find it a little bit too cozy."

On the way home, Matt found himself muttering. "Shrimp. Sardines."

Gina added, "Oranges."

Matt had a thought. "I'd never get this for anyone else for a present since it's so mundane, but I know just the thing to get them for Christmas."

Gina nodded. In chorus, they sang. "Fruit baskets. Lots of fruit baskets."

As usual, it was close to midnight when Dash got together with Chance to go over the day's results in the small conference room by Dash's office. They worked silently side-by-side, marking anomalies in the readouts from the patients' blood work and sensors for deeper analysis. Eventually, Chance remarked casually, "So, just out of curiosity, have you looked at the data on the President for Life to see if he would survive the therapy? I mean, they were all so hot to get you to work on him."

Dash continued making notations. "I did look. It was a

mistake." She peered at the screen intensely for a moment before continuing. "The information is useless."

Chance pushed. "So, would he live or die?"

Dash glowered oppressively. "You don't want to know."

"Of course I do." Chance opened a new window and sought out the President for Life's medical charts.

Dash issued one last warning. "You really don't want to know."

Chance continued to study the charts. Finally, she drew a conclusion. "Aha. Well, isn't that interesting."

"So now that you know, Chance, what are you going to do?"

Chance frowned. "I see what you mean. Should we tell Colin?" She grinned mischievously. "Should we tell the Chief Advisor?"

Dash snorted. "If Colin wanted to know, if there were anything he could do with the information, he would've asked when I updated him on our ability to predict which patients would survive. And as for the Chief Advisor..." She sighed. "Why would he believe us? After all, we have a vested interest. The fact that we are scientists dedicated to truth would have no impact. As Colin pointed out to me, any person who invents his facts as he goes along loses the ability to distinguish actual facts, no matter who is speaking."

Chances nostrils flared, then subsided. "So it really is useless to know."

Dash nodded. "I wish I had not looked."

"Argh." Chance reflected for a moment. "Me neither."

Dash sat back in her chair. "I think we have just about finished here." She raised an eyebrow at Chance. "Is this where I say, 'I told you so'? I am trying to improve my use of English idioms."

Chance just rolled her eyes and started closing windows on the display screen.

There were no jobs in California. None. Nada. So Dennis Gordon, the once proud independent trucker whose truck had been seized for carrying controller chips for SpaceR, had walked from Needles along I-40 to the Arizona border. He still had his Oklahoma driver's license though he had no truck, no home, no money, and no hope.

When he reached the border, he expected a huge hassle from Arizona's not-officially-customs officers. But without his truck, there was no risk he was harboring Mexicans. And since he was obviously a pasty white Caucasian, the Arizona border patrol quickly let him into the state, and even gave him a bottle of water, for which he thanked them.

He had tried hitching a ride, but the cars were all driven by computers even though the trucks still legally required a driver and a steering wheel. Anyway, the computers never stopped for hitchhikers.

So he walked. His water bottle was empty. The sun beat down relentlessly. The austere beauty he had appreciated zooming west with his last truckload of chips now looked desolate and deadly walking east.

He had had the choice of starving to death in California while being berated for having voted Red all these years or dying of thirst in the quiet solitude of the desert. He still thought he'd made the better choice, but it was hard. His mind drifted.

A semi much like his own rolled past, blowing him halfway off the shoulder. Then a classic Corvette, so old it actually needed a human driver, barreled past even faster but started screeching as the driver slammed the brakes. The car pulled onto the shoulder and backed slowly toward him.

For a moment Dennis reconnected with reality, long enough to wonder if this *were* reality any longer. He'd always dreamed of owning a Vette like this one, a 2003 Fiftieth Anniversary convertible. The sunlight shimmered joyfully off the glossily-waxed maroon curves of the machine, built of raw speed and pure power.

The driver's door opened, and a woman in a crisp gold-trimmed white pantsuit stepped out. Why would she stop here?

Dennis finally realized the truth; he had been wrong all along. There *was* in fact an afterlife, and this angel had been sent to take him there. It was fitting, he supposed, that the Corvette he'd once dreamed of should now be the vehicle to carry him into the light.

The angel marched up to him, walking smoothly on the gravel despite her high heels, thus proving her divine provenance. She held a tablet in her hand, which seemed a little less divine, and looked back and forth between the tablet and himself. Was she checking the rolls of the dying to make sure she had the right person?

Having satisfied herself, she addressed him. "Mr. Gordon? My name is Lindsey Postrel. I'm the editor for

Cogent News. Liberated not Regulated. I'm sure you've heard of us." She offered to shake his hand.

Still mesmerized by her Vette and her person, he only caught one word in three. No matter. He placed his hand in hers so she could lead him. "Thank you for coming for me."

She stepped closer and peered into his face. "You're dehydrated," she pronounced crisply. "Let's get you into the car and get you some water."

As she opened the passenger door for him, she tried to explain why she had sought him out. "I understand the Great State of California confiscated your truck. I think you have an important and interesting story to tell."

"Really?" He smiled. "Are they interested in stories about Earth where you're taking me? I hadn't realized."

Jun supervised as the cargo bot lifted Jacques and carried him down the gangway of the *Taixue* onto the artificial beach built between the isle ships. He was so fixated on the proper handling of his bot, he didn't become aware of his audience until he was on the beach.

He was surprised to see how many people were waiting for him.

Professor Thornhill, her arms crossed over her chest, tilted her head ever so slightly in acknowledgment of a job well done. "Bravo, Jun. It looks great." She put her hands on her hips. "You do understand, I hope, that your first test is going to be a disaster. First tests always are."

Ciara, of whom Jun had become quite fond, nudged her

mother. "Don't be such a sourpuss. I think this is going to go just… swimmingly." Her smile made Jun walk taller.

Jun's parents stood to the side watching anxiously. "Is there anything we can help you with?" his father asked.

"No, Dad. I've got this." He said proudly.

Chen Ying frowned with impatience. "Okay, okay, let's get it into the water."

And so the cargo bot dropped Jacques off the beach and into the little patch of partially protected ocean. Jun clamped Jacques' goggles over his face, pulled on the gloves, and started to drive.

Ciara threw a glowing orange tube into the water; it began to sink. "Oh no! I've lost my…stick! Would you get it for me?"

Jun swiveled his head, looking with the eyes of his bot. The orange stick was sinking rapidly out of sight. He accelerated and soon grasped the object. He brought it back to the surface and with a mighty heave threw it back onto the beach. It flew over everyone's heads and hit the side of the *Taixue*. "Oops," Jun said. "Jacques is stronger than I expected"

Chen asked the inevitable question. "So how deep can you go, anyway?"

Jun Laquan did not answer. He simply twisted Jacques so his head pointed down and churned the impellers to full speed. "One hundred meters," he said proudly. "Two hundred meters." He paused. "Three hundred… Oh no."

Ciara clapped. "Almost nine hundred feet! Awesome!" She nudged her mother again and whispered too loudly, "Don't you dare say 'I told you so.'"

Professor Thornhill had her hand over her eyes,

shaking her head. "That was marvelous, Jun. I never would have expected it to go that deep —" she glared at Chen, "— before some idiot urged you to send it so far that we couldn't recover it."

Jun couldn't say anything because he was being hugged too vigorously by his mother. "We are so proud of you," she said glowingly.

Chen Ying threw his hands wide for the professor. "Don't worry, Professor Thornhill. I had him build in automatic buoyancy control. If something breaks, it just comes floating right back to the top of the water." He pointed dramatically at the sea.

He was still pointing dramatically at the sea much later when Jun offered an observation. "We never really tested the automatic recovery system. I'm very sorry." He winced. "We may have actually lost it."

Professor Thornhill put her hand over her eyes again, and just shook her head.

4

———

JOURNEYING

In the Age of gossip-powered media, it is less important to know a lot of facts than to reliably distinguish actual facts from alternative facts.

  -Accel. Topic: Fake News Creation and Identification. Module: Introduction.

Major Zhang of the Chinese People's Liberation Army had to work not to let his shoulders sag. He was a leader of men, so he must look confident and commanding, even when alone, lest some enlisted soldier accidentally walk through the wrong door and see him in a state of imperfect forcefulness.

He sat at his crude metal desk in his immaculately clean but shabby office and looked out his window at the barracks. Well, the troops could use a change of scenery and some brisk marching in unfamiliar territory, no matter how ridiculous the mission.

The governor of the province where he was normally stationed had a first cousin who ran a rehabilitation center for web addicts in the neighboring Shaanxi province. The cousin, unable to get any satisfaction from the governor of his own province, had called his cousin to complain. So now Major Zhang was expected to Do Something.

The major might have laughed about the request, except leaders of men did not laugh, especially about orders given by the governors and the Politburo. He had to take it seriously.

Some Muslim woman, certainly descended from the races west of China, possibly from the BrainTrust, had managed to embarrass the rehab headmaster and run off with one of the inmates—uh, students—of his facility. The loss of the student was no big deal, the headmaster conceded when the major talked to him directly, but ever since then a steady trickle of parents had been streaming in, demanding their children be allowed to take a test on a cell phone app.

The headmaster tried to refuse these demands, but most of the parents were adamant, insisting on the same opportunity to engage their children that Tai's father had demanded. The headmaster could see that if he refused the most determined of them, word would get around and sources of new students would dry up. So he relented, which quickly turned out to be almost as bad: a disturbing number of the parents, upon looking at their children's test results, immediately ripped those children from the disciplined yet nurturing care of the headmaster. They left behind a large and growing number of vacancies with a concomitant loss of profits.

Despite all this, the major had the feeling that the departing students and lost revenues weighed less heavily on the headmaster than whatever the woman had done to him personally. The man practically spluttered as he vented his rage at this unseemly and uncivilized person.

It made no difference. The major was ordered to investigate, and to make a show of force in the process, to discourage others. Fine. A show of force he would give them. After lunch, he packed two trucks with troops and headed out into the backwaters to investigate all the commotion.

The klaxon sounded throughout the *Mount Parnassus*. Ping leaped from her bed with a whoop of delight. "Condition Red!" she announced to no one in particular. She hopped up and down as she pulled on her pants. "Pirates! At last!"

The manufacturing ship for the Fuxing fleet had finally gone operational. Ping's Prometheus fleet had moved to the west, to the eastern coast of Africa on its way around the continent to reach Nigeria on the far side. They'd been using some sort of experimental tech to give the ships a semblance of real speed, but Ping hadn't paid much attention. The tech had mostly worked, breaking down only twice, so they had gotten to Africa in just a couple weeks. They'd just started passing Somalia the night before, and the tech had chosen this moment to break down a third time.

Ping paused as she struggled with the zipper. She continued to talk to herself. "But let's not get too excited just yet. It might be some actual serious problem. But odds are, it's pirates." Her eyes glowed. "Gonna need my Big Gun!" She yanked the door to the cabin open and departed before she'd even finished buttoning her shirt.

Ten minutes later she stood on the top deck of the ship, staring in disgust at the two dinky black Zodiac boats battering themselves against the waves as they bounced to the attack. "That's it? That's all there is?" Ping demanded of the unfair universe. Holding her Big Gun straight in the air, she pressed the unlock button and shook it until it collapsed into its backpack shape.

Putu Arnawa watched her disassemble her beloved weapon in surprise. "Ma'am, aren't we going to shoot them?"

Ping glared, then softened her expression lest he think she was mad at him. "Of course we're going to shoot 'em. But we hardly need the Big Gun. Would you use dynamite to go fishing?"

Suparman Herianto, universally known as Soup, shrugged. "My grandfather always used dynamite. No reason to give the fish a chance, he always said." Soup came from a fishing family in Sumatra. He had grown up on the Brain-Trust after his father had moved to become a reef manager.

Marcos, the last member of her peacekeeping team, made a point. "I suppose we should give them a chance to surrender."

Ping nodded. "Very good." She snapped her phone from her belt. "Captain, please head directly for our attackers."

The captain squawked. "Are you kidding me?"

Ping laughed gaily. "Were you thinking of outrunning

them? At our max speed of four knots? Let's close the distance as quickly as possible. Rescue operations, you know."

A moment's silence held on the phone. "Of course. Anything else?"

"Not right now, Captain." Ping turned to her team. "Putu, get the *Fast Cat* into the water. Soup, I see you brought up our McMillan Tac 50. Good thinking." Ping sighed. "Might as well get in some target practice with the Big Mac." The Big Mac, a .50 caliber sniper rifle known for hitting targets well over a mile away, was also known for its ability to kill engine blocks as well as softer targets. "Soup, set her up, see if you can take out the engine on the lead boat."

Soup objected, "But Ma'am, he's bouncing all over the ocean."

Marcos pointed out, "That's why it's called practice."

Soup popped off five rounds. He missed the engine block entirely, though with the last shot he did blow one of the pirates overboard. "Crap," he muttered, "Sorry."

Ping was watching the Zodiac with a spotter scope. "Occupational hazard," she offered philosophically. She did not specify whether it was a hazard of being a BrainTrust sniper that you might accidentally kill a pirate or a hazard as a pirate that a BrainTrust sniper might kill you. Both, of course, were true.

The pirates pulled their comrade out of the water, looked at his missing chest, and dropped him back in the ocean. With a shake of their fists, they fired an RPG grenade at them that fell far, far short.

Soup grumbled, "I told you they were bouncing all over the place."

Ping agreed cheerfully. "Quite true, Soup. Marcos, let's pick an easier target to soften them up. Just put a couple rounds through the Zodiac's rim." The Zodiac was an inflatable. Each round through the inflatable rim would put two holes in the boat to let the air rush out.

Marcos started shooting. The fourth round hit. He let the boat sink a bit, becoming more sluggish in the water, and fired his last round. Two more holes blew open.

Ping clapped. "My turn. Let's see how it goes with the engine now." She took her time and fired. The outboard motor blew off the boat, almost hitting the second boat, which had slowed down for rescue operations.

Ping switched targets to the second boat. A second shot, and a second engine leaped from its moorings into the sea, burning as it spun across the water. "Soup, put a couple holes in that second boat, just so they understand their situation fully." Ping heard the throaty sound of the high power catamaran engines as Putu brought the *Fast Cat* out to the dock. "Meanwhile, I'll go with Putu and see what kind of fish we can pick out of the sea."

The *Fast Cat* was *fast*. They reached the wallowing pirate craft in a few minutes. One of the pirates lifted his RPG launcher at them, then lifted off his feet and went backward over the side of the boat, taking the launcher with him. Ping held her hand high in a thumbs up for Marcos back on the Parnassus. "Two down, six to go," Ping said to no one in particular.

The rest of the pirates showed good judgment and picked up no other weapons. Ping took the helm while

Putu, who was considerably huskier than herself, helped the survivors onto the catamaran.

———

The sun fell across the terraced landscape of northern China as Jam pulled her "new" LandWind to the side of the road. She'd thought her Range Rover was a battered junk heap, but now she looked back upon it with a fondness generally reserved for Maseratis. Her present LandWind, a Chinese home-built knockoff of the Rover, had been dilapidated a hundred thousand miles earlier. She had no words in either Pashtun or English for its current state of disrepair. The seats were so badly ripped that duct tape no longer held the leather together. Rather, the occasional strip of leather held the duct tape in place.

They had driven back to the Loess Plateau almost nonstop. They had made small detours twice to investigate reports of people passing the Accel test. One young man had been sent on to the Fuxing, while another had failed the in-person assessment. Other than that, Jam and Julissa had paused only to switch drivers and pump gas. Exhaustion had consumed her very bones. She knew she had been even wearier during her desperate journey to seek out the BrainTrust, but that had been several lifetimes ago, and her memories of that time had softened.

At least this time bleak despair did not color her mood. This was more like her time in the commandos, when she knew that if she just continued to put one foot in front of the other, eventually she would arrive.

And arrive she had. Having seen Song, Tai, and Xiu's

parents off on their journey to Vietnam, she was now only a few kilometers away from where she had first met Song, traveling on to the next family of candidates that had been identified by the Accel app. They had a mere a hundred kilometers left to go to pick up where they had left off.

But they would do that tomorrow. Julissa was in no better shape than she was, her eyes glazed with fatigue. The two of them fell asleep in their seats by the side of the road.

Jam dozed fitfully; her dreams passed into remembrance as she thought about the last conversation she'd had with Ping as she'd departed on this crazy expedition:

They had stood on the gangway to the ferry hugging goodbye, as Ping had been trying to teach Dash to do. Then Ping took one step back and transformed, for the second time since Jam had met her, into a serious person, an owlish analyst of unwavering intensity.

Ping squeezed Jam's shoulders. "When you get into the North, on the Loess Plateau, look for a town named Baotong."

Jam pulled out her tablet. "Baotong?" She brought up the GPlex Maps app.

Ping snorted. "Baotong. Don't bother looking on any maps, the town is much too small and far too forgotten."

Jam was tempted to ask how Ping knew about it if it had been forgotten but figured she wouldn't get a straight answer. "How do I find it, then?"

"When you get to the area, ask around among the

people in the other small villages. Someone should be able to point you in the right direction."

Jam looked at her skeptically. "Seems like a lot of trouble, unless there's someone there who belongs on the BrainTrust." She worked her display to show Ping a map of the Loess Plateau with a scattering of dots denoting places where people had passed the Accel test, hoping to join the Fuxing. "Are any of these dots in Baotong?"

Ping shook her head morosely. "They don't even have cell phones there, Jam." She pursed her lips. "Just do what I tell you. Trust me on this. You'll find what you're looking for if you find Baotong."

Ping's eyes turned wild; the analyst was lost once more. "You're taking your dress, aren't you?"

Jam rolled her eyes. "I have no idea why, but yes, I'm taking my gown from First Launch." When she and Ping had arrived at their new quarters in the Prometheus fleet and the Fuxing fleet respectively, each had found the dresses they'd rented for just one day. Each came with a note from Dash, *After the party, Daniella offered them to me at an incredible price, since otherwise, she would have just thrown them out. I thought you might have better use for them.*

"Good, good. I just know you're going to knock somebody off their feet with that gown." Ping had laughed and waved as Jam's ferry set off for Hong Kong.

The dreams and memories dissolved abruptly just before dawn. Jam awoke to the sound of a passing pickup truck, green, shiny, and newer than anything she had seen in days. She put the LandWind in gear and followed.

Few roads interconnected in this land of desolation. The fact that the green pickup seemed to be going to the same place she was going did not stir any suspicions…until the truck turned right in the middle of a village onto the same dirt track her GPS had told her to follow. When the truck stopped at a hovel moments before her GPS told her that she had arrived, she felt no surprise whatsoever. Jam smiled grimly. When she had called Dash to ask if she had any ideas for better backcountry transportation, had Dash sent her this vehicle? It did not seem high tech enough to be Dash's idea of a solution, though it was certainly practical.

According to the testing app, the family living here had two children, sixteen and thirteen, who made good candidates. She could see them now, running out of their dwelling and rushing over to see the shiny truck, no doubt far superior to anything that had ever parked by their house before.

But the truck itself quickly lost its luster as the primary attraction. The sixteen-year-old, tall enough to see over the side of the pickup into the truck bed, started pointing excitedly; he lifted his younger sister so she could see it as well, and together their excitement burst to new heights. Their enthusiasm suggested to Jam that perhaps the gift Dash had sent her was neither so simple nor so practical as she had supposed.

Jam strolled over to the truck, smiling warmly as she waved to the parents standing beneath a shallow awning watching their children. Looking into the truck bed, her heart skipped a beat. A huge assemblage of parts greeted her. Parts that could only be helicopter propellers gave her her first sensation of dread.

Was this a homebrew copter straight from the Brain-Trust laser tag games, delivered as a do-it-yourself kit? Jam had to confess, she didn't really enjoy flying. Sure, she had learned to parachute during her time as a commando, but jumping out of a perfectly good airplane with nothing but a parachute still seemed insane to her. Only one thing seemed more insane: stepping into an airplane of uncertain perfection *without* a parachute.

The children had no such qualms. The father, who had left his wife behind, smiled broadly. "Are you the tester from the BrainTrust?" He hardly seemed interested in the answer; perhaps the answer was obvious. He had a more immediate purpose. "It looks like you have a copter here." He scrutinized the plethora of parts. "More likely two copters, I think. Any chance you could build them here so we can see? Maybe even take a ride?"

A teenager jumped out of the driver's side of the green truck. "Are you Jam? I have a form here for you to fill out. Do you want the truck as well? They told me to give you the truck too if you wanted it." He thrust a tablet in her face.

Jam sighed in relief. At least she'd gotten the truck too, in addition to whatever the truck carried. She signed the forms for the driver, who swiped a document from his tablet over to hers. Only then did the ex-driver look around at the scenery with horror. "Now all I have to do is figure out how to get home."

Jam smiled; she had an answer. "Take the LandWind."

He looked doubtful.

Jam shrugged. "It's taken us thousands of kilometers. Believe it or not, it'll probably get you home. Worst case, you'll still be better off wherever you are when it dies."

The teenager seemed to accept that. He grabbed her keys, helped Julissa empty their luggage, and took off in a cloud of small rocks and dust.

Meanwhile, the father was still expecting her answer about the copters. Jam frowned. "Honestly, this is the first time I've ever seen these. I have no idea how to put them together."

The son practically jumped up and down. "We can build it!" He looked at his father, then at Jam, then back again. "I'm sure we can build it!" His sister nodded in agreement.

The father frowned at them. "I think you'll need a little help." He smiled. "I think if I helped you, you'd have a better chance." He looked questioningly at Jam.

Jam looked at the sky. The father hid his enthusiasm better, but he wanted to build the copters as much as his children did. "Very well." She looked down at the doc, which was labeled *Assembly Instructions*. "You'll need this." She handed him the tablet.

His wife still stood under the awning, arms folded over her chest. As the children let down the tailgate, the mother came over to greet Jam and Julissa in her turn. "Would you like some tea while my family is busy with this contraption?"

Julissa bobbed a partial bow. "That would be most welcome."

So Jam sat under the awning, sipping white tea, watching as two copters of a new design took shape. The husband brought her tablet back to her. "I think we've got it from here."

She took the tablet and began to read the main message, clearly a note from Dash. *Jam, sorry this took so long. As you may be able to tell, we've sent you two copters that I think will help you considerably in your mission.* Jam had been thinking about what to do with the darn things the whole time she'd been watching their construction. In the end, she concluded they might actually be quite useful. She could plant the truck with their luggage at a less disreputable hotel in a larger village and pop out to examine the Accel applicants all over the region before returning at night. She might not like flying, but she certainly did like speed, at least for this mission.

She continued to read. *Even before you called I had been working with Ted, the teenage copter inventor who rescued me from Dmitri's yacht, on some ideas for you. I fear he had more ideas then we could fit into a single copter design. Ever since we got shot down by that Russian assault helicopter—* what!? Somebody had used an assault helicopter to shoot at Dash?! Jam hadn't heard that part of the story. Somebody needed some personal rehabilitation on proper behavior— *Ted has been fixated on "militarizing" his copter designs. And his favorite customer, Matt Toscano—you may remember him from the party—has been encouraging him.* Jam closed her eyes briefly. She now dreaded to see the fine print on the operation of the copters.

Anyway, you now have the first two stealth copters ever built on the BrainTrust. It seems my friends with this startup specializing in graphene applications ran into some old research on applying electrical voltages to graphene to absorb different elec-

tromagnetic frequencies. So there's a switch on the control panel that allows you to turn on "stealth mode" that will absorb just about all radar waves.

Between the black graphene copter surface, the radar absorption, and the catalytic fuel burners that convert the energy directly into electricity, thus circumventing infrared detection, your copters can be pretty much invisible. Especially at night.

Of course, the stealth is still a little bit experimental, so try not to depend on it too much. Jam had to look away for a moment to get calm. Being "a little bit experimental" was, she had learned, quite similar to being a little bit pregnant.

Anyway, the engines are very efficient, so these are also longer-range than most BrainTrust helicopters. Just be thankful I told Ted to hurry and get these out to you. Otherwise, you'd have had to wait a while longer while he tried to integrate bullet-proofing as well. Jam chuckled. She could just hear Dash lecturing some teenager on scheduling.

Regardless, I confess I feel more comfortable having sent you these. I cannot help fearing that the tyrants of China will be displeased with your efforts. It gives me great peace of mind knowing you can escape easily at any time, completely disappearing from their view. Jam appreciated the sentiment.

I don't know if you know how to fly a copter. They're mostly automated, of course, but you really should know how to operate the controls. There are a pair of switches on the dashboard for virtual training mode. You should spend an hour or two practicing before taking it into the air.

Jam looked up to see a commotion by the first copter, apparently now fully built. The son had clearly climbed aboard, flipped on the virtual training mode, and taken it for a virtual flight. Now the father and daughter were bickering over who got to try it next. The mother intervened; the little girl climbed into the cockpit. The father turned to Jam and shouted above the chaos, "once we've all taken the training, can we take it up?"

The little girl, though she had not yet met Lenora, seemed to have learned one of her lessons at a tender age: *'Tis better to ask forgiveness than beg permission.* A soft whir arose from the copter as the child-pilot set the props to spinning up. The father started yelling in consternation. Loose dirt swirled as the copter wobbled into the air.

Yes, these people would make excellent BrainTrust members. They already fit in.

Jam looked back down at Dash's message. *Lastly, once you're comfortable flying the copters, please call me. I have a favor to ask of you.* In the middle of northern China? What could she possibly want?

Love, Dash. "Love you too, girl," Jam muttered.

5

TWO CHOCOLATES

Here we investigate both Alt-Right and Alt-Left cookbooks for manufacturing alternative facts in support of fantasy belief systems. All alternative fact systems follow the basic SAD principles that drive successful popular media: keep it Simple, keep it Angry, keep it Divisive.

—Accel. Topic: Fake News Creation and Identification. Module: Introduction.

Ping leaned forward in her chair, her brow furrowed. "Are you sure Diric can't qualify? Can't you test him a little more to be sure?"

Ciara lifted a cup of jasmine tea to her lips and put it down without drinking. It needed to cool.

They were alone in the cafeteria, not unusual given their skeleton crew. Actually, with most of the work being done by the bots, even a traditional skeleton crew would have been considered extensive in comparison with the number of crewmen now driving the Prometheus fleet.

Ciara raised an eyebrow. "Ping, why is this so important to you? He's a pirate, he tried to kidnap us."

Ping waved it away. "His uncle, who raised him after his parents died, tried to kidnap us. The uncle's dead. Diric had very little in the way of choices when his uncle told him to come along."

Ciara looked at her doubtfully. She didn't even have to counter verbally for Ping to know the answer: *we always have a choice.*

Ping sighed. "He has nowhere else to go with his uncle dead."

Ciara sipped the tea carefully. "As soon as we catch up with that Danish patrol ship he's going to prison, so it's not really an issue."

"Where he'll learn nothing but how to be a better pirate. Besides..." Ping mumbled unintelligibly.

"What was that again?"

Ping hunched over as if the next words hurt. "Besides, I kinda like him. He's a good kid."

Ciara laughed, almost snorting the tea through her nose. "Ok, ok. Just for that, I'll give him one more test. He's almost bright enough anyway, it would be good to have at least one student rattling around in this fleet made for twenty thousand." She looked at Ping sternly. "But only if he passes the test."

Ping straightened up and nodded sharply. "Of course. S'all I ask."

Ping watched from the observation room as Ciara led Diric into a tiny barren conference room: it was the same room used to run the Milgram protocols, though it was not configured for that today. Ciara looked straight into the camera at Ping as she unlocked his shackles: Ping could not tell whether the glare meant, "I hope you're right about this," or "You better be in here instantly if he attacks me." Of course, Diric was such a skinny little thing it was hard to imagine him being dangerous, but Ping of all people knew full well how dangerous skinny little things could be.

Ciara started chatting with Diric ever so casually. When he relaxed, she pulled a pair of chocolates from her pocket. "Here," she said, sliding one over to him, "have one."

He took a small bite of the chocolate, ever so skeptically, then his eyes lit up and he swallowed the rest of it almost without chewing. You never would have guessed he'd been getting the fullest meals of his life for the last few days here on *Mount Parnassus*.

Ciara finished chewing hers, clearly relishing it. She pulled out another chocolate, slid it halfway over to him, then made a big fuss searching her pockets for another one. "I seem to be out of chocolates." She tapped the chocolate on the table. "If you can wait for me to get back before eating this one, I'll bring you another."

Moments later Ciara joined Ping in the observation room. They both stared at Diric, staring at the lone chocolate, desperate desire imprinted on his mournful face.

Ping shook her head. "You and your mother have the strangest ways of testing people."

Ciara chuckled. "This is called 'The Two Chocolate Test.' At the very beginning of the century, researchers discovered that children who can delay gratification and wait for the second chocolate are more likely to lead successful adult lives." She looked at Ping. "If he passes the test, he's yours." She shrugged. "And mine too. They're all mine, I guess, on the Prometheus."

Ping watched tensely as Diric stared at the chocolate. He wiped his brow. Ping wiped her brow as well.

Again Ciara laughed. "Perhaps you should turn away. I think the test is stressing you more than Diric."

Even as she spoke, Diric turned away from his chocolate to stare at the wall. After a moment, he closed his eyes. His nostrils flared as if he could still smell his own personal nemesis. Finally, he visibly relaxed.

Ciara clapped. "And that's it, folks." She put her hand on Ping's shoulder. "Anyone who can turn away from the chocolate and think about something else can wait forever. He's golden, Ping, good to go." She reached into her pocket and gave Ping a chocolate. "Why don't you take him his reward, and welcome him to the BrainTrust?"

Ping stared at the candy in her hand. "Wait. Don't I get a chocolate too?"

Ciara glared and pointed imperiously to the door.

Fan swept into the brig, demanding to see Guang. The guard looked at her with bemusement, since he'd already received orders to release the prisoner. Fan went to his cell and yanked the door open.

Guang had been dozing on his bunk. He opened his eyes and smiled in a way that was almost sincere. "You finally got me out of this place? Good girl." He winced as he joined her. His broken rib had mostly healed, but still complained when he shifted the wrong way. "I can't believe they locked me up like an animal and wouldn't even let me talk to anybody. When I tell my father, he's going to blow this place sky high."

Fan suppressed the urge to point out that that was exactly the reason Lenora hadn't allowed him to talk to anyone. She and Lenora had strategized on how to get him back to China without causing any fatal incidents. Fan thought the plan they'd concocted was pretty good, though from Fan's perspective it was a very irritating plan. Her boyfriend was such a child. An irredeemable child, she had realized of late. "As a personal thing, I would appreciate it if you would avoid blowing this ship up, at least while I'm still on it. I think Chen's mother might object as well."

"Of course, of course, we'll have to evacuate Chen first." Guang waved the objection away, then gasped as the motion drove a flare of pain through his chest.

Fan held to her poker face. She thought about how interesting it would be to punch her boyfriend in the ribs, to see how much reaction she could get. But this was no time for daydreams. "Come on. I have a copter waiting to take us back to the mainland."

"Excellent. The sooner we're home, the sooner we can get justice."

———

Fan had taken the copter into the air and pushed it to its fastest cruising speed before Guang returned to his topic of the day, namely, revenge. "What happened to that little bitch that assaulted me?"

"The one that put you in the hospital?" Damn, she had not intended to egg him on like that. She had to keep better control of her reactions.

Guang clenched his fist. "That one. She needs to be executed."

"No need. She's been expelled from the Fuxing." The peacekeeper, Ping, Fan remembered the name, was presumably Chinese though no one seemed sure. Fan saw no need to tell Guang that Ping's "expulsion" was a simple matter of continuing her original mission.

He brightened. "No kidding?"

"No kidding. She's been sent off with the Prometheus archipelago. They're going around Africa. She'll probably wind up fighting pirates." Fan had not met Ping, but everyone talked about how she yearned to fight pirates.

Guang's eyes glinted with malice. "Hopefully they'll give her what she deserves."

Fan took a breath. "I have every confidence they'll give her what she deserves." At least she could agree with that easily.

A companionable silence followed but quickly ended. Guang patted his pockets in growing frustration. "Damn. We left without getting my cell phone back. I wanted to call ahead and get Xiu Bao's parents arrested. I wanted to have them in custody by the time we landed."

Fat chance of that. Fan had been there when Lenora got word that the parents were safely in Vietnam, headed to the Fuxing. That phone call had triggered the release of Guang from the brig.

Guang was still speaking. "I don't suppose I could use your phone?"

"Even if I gave it to you, it wouldn't do you any good." She pointed out the cockpit canopy in all directions; around them was nothing but empty ocean and clear sky as far as the eye could see. "We're way outside cell phone coverage, Guang. Nobody can hear us now."

Guang's eyes focused on the control panel. "What about using the copter radio?"

Fan shook her head. "Lenora would never let me fly the copter again if I used it for anything other than flight operations."

Guang tapped his fingernails against his armrest. He brightened as a thought came to him. "We have a cruiser just a few kilometers away from the Fuxing, right? We could radio them to start the assault on the archipelago. That would surely qualify as flight operations. I'm sure the captain would take orders from me."

Fan found this a bit naïve. Once upon a time, she would have found it charmingly so. How cute. Now it just made her impatient. She explained the problem from a different angle. Again. "Chen Ying."

Guang nodded. "Right. Forgot." He sat for a time, just studying her face as the copter hummed along. "Are you angry at me? What could you be angry at me for?"

Fan did not scream. "Yes, Guang, I'm very angry with you."

He looked completely baffled. "Surely you're not angry at me about that little peasant girl. It's not like she was the first one." Another thought struck him. "Were you afraid I might damage one of your assets?"

Fan waved the question away. "No, no. Chinese peasant girls are sturdy. She would've been fine." Fan had been trying to figure out how to explain the problem for days but had failed to figure out any way of explaining it that Guang might understand. She just blurted it out. "It's just that we had this place wired. They needed us so much." Specifically, Fan had thought that the BrainTrusters needed them so much they would have had to allow Guang to graduate no matter how much he screwed up. Though after working with Lenora for a while she realized her original expectations for bulldozing the BrainTrusters had probably been over-optimistic. "But you managed to find the way to make them kick you out anyway. You knew this place was run by squeamish Westerners. You should've known they would never let this go. How could you have been such an idiot?"

This left Guang speechless for a satisfying length of time. Finally, the Chinese coast rose on the horizon.

Guang lifted an eyebrow. "Hong Kong? I expected we'd go to Shanghai. I don't like Hong Kong."

Of course, he didn't. The people in Hong Kong did not kneel to his every whim. They constantly forgot they were just a part of the Chinese empire. Fan even sympathized with the periodic motions in the Politburo to conduct a proper purge of the city, to bring the people of Hong Kong the discipline they lacked. She sighed. Irrelevant. "We're going inland a bit. Foshan."

"Foshan?"

Fan smiled grimly. He would understand, sort of, soon enough.

Twilight had fallen by the time they finally descended.

Fan dropped the copter into the center of a street intersection. People honked and swerved and swore; a policeman strolled over, fuming; she explained who she was; he set to work putting up roadblocks to move traffic around her impromptu-but-now-official parking space. Guang opened his door, got halfway out, then looked at her quizzically. "You coming?"

Fan took a deep breath. "No, Guang, I'm not coming. I'm taking the copter back to the archipelago. It's theirs, you know." She reached under her seat and pulled out a huge roll of cash. "For you. Compensation for damages." She refrained from mentioning it was also a partial refund of his unused tuition.

His hands automatically took the money, but his mind was clearly not on the task. "How am I supposed to get home from here? I still don't have my phone." He frowned petulantly.

"You can make a call from there." She pointed at a large building brilliantly outlined in neon lights. "You might want to stay there tonight and start home in the morning."

He looked where her finger pointed. His expression softened.

"I have to go, Guang. Catch you another day." Fan leaned far out from the pilot's chair to pull the passenger door closed, but Guang paid no attention. He was already in motion towards his night's lodging. Fan watched to make sure he made it all the way into the building before spinning up her propellers.

Foshan had been the first city under Communist rule to declare prostitution legal back in the late twentieth century. In recent years, the city had upped its game in the industry. Guang would now be comfortably ensconced in the brothel reputed to be number one in the province. In addition to the usual Vietnamese and Chinese girls, the place had recently acquired a stable of young Russian women. Guang would like that.

Fan was quite sure he was receiving a royal reception at this moment. She and Lenora had called ahead to make sure of it. By the time he ran out of cash and remembered he needed a phone several days from now, he would have hopefully cooled off. She doubted even Guang's father would authorize a military assault on the archipelago just because they'd kicked him out of school yet again, but best not to leave it to chance.

As she took the copter aloft, she yelled at the building he'd entered. "Guang, you're just too stupid to be a good boyfriend!" There. That made her feel better. As she headed home to the Fuxing, she daydreamed about hitting him in the ribs just once, just for the satisfaction of it.

Equal Injustice for All
—Lindsey Postrel, Cogent News

"Don't do the crime if you can't do the time," was once a sensible attitude to take about breaking the law. But as we have learned from Dennis Gordon (see the picture of Dennis below, near death from exposure on the open highway after being stripped of all his belongings by California State Police), you don't have to do any real crime to be punished. But fear not, because you still don't have to do the time—you just have to watch the State

take everything else from you. And I do mean everything. Take Dennis for example...

Lowly out of state peons like Dennis are not the only ones who lose everything to the rapacious needs of the state. Equal injustice for all has finally been achieved in California. One percenters here are now more likely, on a per capita basis, to be stripped of all their belongings with civil forfeiture than the ordinary man on the street.

Indeed, the state's Attorney General maintains a list of millionaires to be stripped whenever the state budget risks going into the red. Cogent has obtained a copy of this fascinating document and attached it to the bottom of the article. If you are on the list, hurry. It may already be too late.

For those of you in my readership who have more money than the average bear, even if you're not on the list, it is time to take heed and take this advice: get out now.

Lenora sagged in her chair, a La-Z-Boy office chair with both the headrest and a kick-out footrest. She knew from past experience that the chair was easy to sleep in. But now, at the end of the day, she was not sleepy, merely tired.

There was good news and bad news about being an Accel teacher. Her whole day was devoted to helping children overcome the most difficult obstacles to the next steps in their education. This led to both the good news and the bad. The good news was, it was far more gratifying than giving a rote lecture to a class where only half the students were paying attention, a quarter of them were falling asleep, and the rest were whispering, giggling, and fidgeting. The bad news was, it was exhausting in that special way that occurred when your brain was taxed to the limit.

Lenora had just closed her eyes and taken a deep breath when she heard a knock on her door. "Come on in," she said as heartily as she could considering how much she wanted to be left alone.

Jun Laquan came in, followed by Chen Ying…followed by Song and then by Xiu Bao. Chen had told Lenora that Jun's team of engineers had gotten larger. "Jacques the scuba bot" had become so famous it was practically a class project. Now Jun's team was so large it barely fit in her office.

Jun proudly held out the 3-D goggles and haptic feed-back gloves used to operate the bot. "We just reached the ocean floor," he crooned.

Chen continued. "We thought you deserved to be one of the first people to check it out."

Everyone watched her anxiously as she pulled on the shoulder length gloves and slipped on the goggles. Before her view of the room was completely occluded by the view from the bottom of the sea, she saw that Jun had slaved her wallscreen to the goggles so everyone could see at least a 2D representation

In her goggles, she could see a brilliantly lit circle of sea bottom surrounded by inky blackness. A couple of tiny lights winked at an indeterminate distance, presumably the bioluminescence given off by some of the denizens of the deep sea. She extended her arms as if she were going to fly, Superman-style, and the bot started briskly forward. Moving her hands back and forth, she was able to turn.

When she pulled her arms back, the bot slowed to hover a few feet off the bottom.

Lenora found that moving her head around caused the lights to track in the direction she looked. Off to her right, she saw a smooth surfaced egg-shaped rock. At least she thought it was a rock. Without conscious thought, she moved her hands towards the rock, and the bot went to the object. She grasped it, and the feedback through the gloves told her that indeed it was a rock, not a sponge or something else soft or squishy. "What is this?" she asked of her attentive audience, though she had a suspicion she knew exactly what it was.

Xiu answered excitedly. "It's a manganese nodule. I've read about them. They're supposed to be valuable, but they're too expensive to retrieve."

Lenora smiled. It was very strange, smiling for what you knew to be a room full of people when all you could see was a rock held in sturdy mechanical hands in the middle of a tiny circle of light. "So, I don't think it would be very expensive to bring this one up to see if you're right. Jun, how would we bring this home?"

Jun answered excitedly, "You should be able to just hold the rock way out in front of you with both hands, tilt your arms up, and come back to the surface. Here, let me."

Jun did something that caused the robot to lock in position while they traded the goggles and the gloves.

Song observed, "You'd better hurry, I don't know that you've actually got enough power left to bring both Jacques and the egg back to the surface."

Chen answered. "Worst case, the automatic recovery system kicks in." He paused. "That might not be enough to bring the rock up as well, though. Jun, you should probably force the recovery system to start now."

Jun shifted his hands to hold the egg like a football, then twisted his free fingers in an odd little dance that presumably triggered the recovery system.

Chen explained. "An emergency battery, just for the recovery system, is now electrolyzing the seawater and filling two internal balloons, one with hydrogen and one with oxygen."

Lenora, along with everyone else, could see on the wallscreen that the bot was rising at an accelerating pace.

A commotion at the door caused Song and Xiu to move aside for someone else, catching Lenora's attention.

Qi Ru, the hukou peasant who had gone to Oxford, earned a fortune in high finance, and come to the Fuxing to run a venture funding brokerage, stuck his head in. "Did I hear someone say they'd found something valuable?"

As Xiu explained about the manganese nodules that contained multiple valuable elements, Qi Ru nodded excitedly. "So, can we collect these precious eggs off the sea bottom cheaply enough to be useful?"

Song shrugged. "Don't see why not. Except, I guess, for the manpower we'd need to drive all those bots."

Chen Ying answered. "Not a problem. Give me a little time and I can develop software to find and collect the nodules."

Qi Ru rubbed his hands together as he looked at Lenora. "See? I told you there'd be opportunity here."

Lenora rolled her eyes. If she hadn't expected a lot of opportunities here, she never would have proposed this venture to the BrainTrust Consortium in the first place.

And then she realized that there might be yet another opportunity here besides just making the revenues that would make these archipelagos viable. Her smile brightened as she contemplated another idea she could not share with the others.

6

PERFECTLY LEGAL

Nine people live on island A and one person lives on island B. The people of island A unanimously vote to disallow using resources on island B, including the person on B. Explain the moral hazards and the likely destructive consequences. Identify two alternative incentive systems that produce better long-term outcomes.

—Accel. Topic: Incentive Engineering. Module: Macro-Incentives.

The governor of the Great Blue State of California looked at the news page and groaned. He handed his tablet to the attorney general. "I think we've suffered a serious leak."

The attorney general took the tablet and scanned the article. He was shaking as he returned it to the governor. "'Cogent News' my eye. All she ever reports are facts. She has no idea what truth is, or how much more important it is than mere facts. Well, the good news is, nobody reads her damn rant sheet anyway."

The governor tapped his tablet. "You're almost right," he conceded. "Very few people read Ms. Postrel's rants. Unfortunately, about half the people on our civil forfeiture priority list are among her tiny readership, and the rest have friends who read that damn rant sheet."

The attorney general's face froze in place. He hastily opened his own tablet and started working through a number of queries. "Goddammit!" he screamed. "You're right. And they've already started leaving." He shook his head. "Well, there's no help for it. We have to move into civil forfeiture proceedings immediately against all the ones we can still get our hands on." A gleam entered his eye. "And we're going to start with that damned Toscano bastard. He moved his money out of the state when he moved out SpaceR's funds, but he still has a house in Palos Verdes."

The governor shook his head. "Too late. They sold it almost a week ago. They took a smaller than typical profit on it if that's any consolation. But it's almost as if, after we seized the SpaceR factory, Toscano figured his house would be next." The governor tried to maintain good humor and continued, "Can't imagine why he'd think that."

The governor rose from his desk and went to his bar for a scotch and water. "Believe it or not, we have a bigger problem."

The attorney general stared at him in utter bafflement.

"With some judicious cuts we can probably squeak through this year without a budgetary crisis, but only if our costs don't go up dramatically. Unfortunately, the Red media have picked up on Postrel's story. So it's not just loons wanting factual news who know what we're doing. All the independent truckers who bring goods into the state have heard about it. They've stopped coming in-state. Some sort of driver association is demanding that Dennis get his truck back before they'll make any more deliveries. The California truckers' union is happily offering to pick up the slack, going all over the nation to pick up goods, but—"

"No!" The attorney general turned pale. "We can't afford that!"

"We certainly can't. Glad you see the problem."

The attorney general joined him at the minibar for a shot of straight whiskey. "I guess we could set up transfer stations at all the major border crossings. The independent truckers could drop their loads at the border, California union drivers hitch 'em up and carry them the rest of the way. It'll still cost more, but it won't be exorbitant."

The governor closed his eyes for a moment. He hated asking the following question, for which he already knew the Attorney General's answer. "I don't suppose we could just give this Dennis fellow his truck back? And back off on the civil forfeitures for a while?"

The attorney general stared, just speechless for a moment. The governor's mantra might be, "Get ahead of the media and stay there," but the attorney general's mantra was simpler: "Once you've got the money, never give it back." His answer to the governor, of course, had nothing to do with his mantra. "Governor, giving the truck back is absolutely unworkable. It would be an admission of guilt. Which is crazy. We haven't done anything wrong. It's all been perfectly legal."

The governor opened his mouth as if to object, but then thought better of it and instead took a sip of his Scotch.

Major Zhang took little joy in terrorizing the peasants as he had been ordered. He had made sure his troops didn't enjoy it too much either. Other commanders might take joy in stirring up a little rebellion for the sake of having the opportunity to put it down, but not he.

Still, he had obeyed orders. He had done a little terrorizing while rumbling about the countryside in search of the disruptive interloper. She seemed to have disappeared from the province, however, along with the father and the son on whose behalf she had intervened. He could track them down, of course, unless they'd left China. China might have over a billion people, but it had over two billion surveillance cameras. No one could escape the eagle eye of the State.

But tracking down the foreigner and her proteges did not seem worth the effort. They no longer represented a threat to the state. Looking at the father's social credit rating, Zhang couldn't help thinking the province was better off without him. Let someone else deal with his disrespectful attitude.

He had turned the trucks around, loaded the troops, and stepped into the passenger's side of the lead truck when his phone demanded his attention. The headmaster again. Argh. "Major Zhang here. How may I help you?"

The headmaster spluttered in poorly controlled anger. "I hear you're leaving without having found her."

"She's gone, sir. Apparently, she departed the day after your encounter with her."

"Well, she's back again. She's giving joy rides in an illegal helicopter."

An illegal helicopter? That sounded interesting if nothing else. It might be worth checking out. Perhaps he could persuade the dastardly villainess to give him a ride home in the copter, letting the troops find their way back without him. Though that might make the wrong impression. Still... "Why are you so certain that this copter is being operated by the same person?"

The headmaster hesitated for a moment before answering. "What are the odds that two different foreign women would stir up trouble out in this backwater at almost the same time?"

The major had to concede the headmaster made an excellent point. "We'll check it out," he promised.

He still wasn't exactly sure what to do about it if he found the woman who had stolen the headmaster's prisoner. She hadn't actually broken any law, and he had considerable personal sympathy for anyone who tweaked the headmaster's nose. If she really did have a copter, and it really was illegal, he would mete out punishment that would satisfy his superiors. If not, he might find himself just offering to buy her a drink. Hmmm... Mission. Duty. Honor. Not necessarily in that order, however, he found himself thinking.

Dash held the door to her office open for Ben, carefully masking the dismay she felt as she watched him shuffle in on his walker, now accompanied by a nursing bot. He was deteriorating with astonishing speed. She took a deep breath, acknowledging to herself it was foolish to be surprised. The speed of his deterioration was, after all, what Dark Alpha had implied when it said Ben had only three weeks left to live. That was the reason she was taking this exceptional step.

Ben maneuvered to the chair next to her small table, and the nursing bot lifted him gently from his walker and set him down. Dash sat down across from him.

His body might be dying, but his eyes were still alive. He spoke in a wheezy voice. "Dash, it's always so wonderful to see you. I confess I hope you asked me in to share some good news."

Dash sighed. "I do not know if it is good news or not. Chance has come up with a radical idea for how to give you a small amount of rejuvenation." It disturbed her that Chance was the one who had come up with it. Radical as it was, it was also obvious. Dash considered it a grave failure on her part to have not come up with the idea herself. She probably needed to back off on helping Matt and Rhett and the others with their projects. She needed to focus.

"Wonderful!" Ben paused. "Uh, what are the chances that I will die in the process?"

"The chances are a hundred percent that you will die. The interesting question is, what are the chances that we can bring you back? This will be as much a reincarnation as a rejuvenation."

Ben sat back in his chair. "Aha. I can see why you're not sure whether the news is good."

"Exactly so." Dash reached out and gently touched his hand with her fingertips. "I would not suggest it were your situation not so dire." She smiled mischievously. "I need to do my best to protect my funding sources, after all."

Ben waved it away. "I know I'm still your biggest investor, but let's face it. You made enough profits from the successful rejuvenations at this point to be self-funding. You don't actually need me anymore."

"Perhaps not. But there will no doubt be other ventures in the future, and I would not like to have to break in another partner."

Ben started to laugh, but it turned into a wracking cough. "Well played, Dash." He looked at her more seriously than he had ever looked at her before. "When do we start?"

"Now, Ben. Right now."

***

Dash stood over him by the bed and held his hand while Chance gave him the injection. Dash explained, "This is a much more aggressive version of our most recent therapy. You will not be immune to it."

Chance continued the explanation. "The current normal version of the therapy has twice as good a chance to rejuvenate the patient as the version you received in the very first test. For a randomly selected candidate, that version gives a fifty-fifty chance of getting younger on the one hand, or dying on the other."

A hopeful expression filled Ben's face. "So I have a fifty-fifty chance?"

Dash let him see her dismay. "No. You are not a random patient, and this is a much more aggressive version than normal. We have successfully characterized the patients who will live and who will die."

Chance joined in with a chipper note in her voice. "As I think Dash told you earlier, you have a hundred percent chance of dying. Since this is even more aggressive, you'd be even more sure of dying, if that were possible."

Ben shook his head. "I see. I know you told me so, but somehow I just couldn't quite bring myself to believe it."

Dash glared at Chance, then spoke to Ben. "Because it is so aggressive, even you will respond to the therapy. As you die, your cells will be infused with the ability to replace themselves with younger versions."

Ben gave her a wheezing laugh. "Perhaps I can be a good-looking corpse."

Chance shook her head. "You'll be dead before they have a chance to start replacing themselves." Her eyes gleamed. "That's when the exciting and fun part begins."

Ben looked so pale and ghastly, Dash held up her hand in a stopping motion. "Enough," she said to Chance sternly. "I don't know that Ben can take much more cheerful explanation." She flickered a light between Ben's eyes to check his pupils. Then she glanced at the monitors. "It has begun."

Both women sat quietly, one on each side of Ben's bed, watching the monitors. Occasionally, Dash would gesture and specify a drug, and Chance would add it to his intravenous drip. Soon enough, Ben started breathing in short, painful gasps. "Oh my. This seems to be the painful part. I'd heard about what happened to the other patients who died, who chose lethal injections rather than live with the pain anymore." He closed his eyes and winced. "I don't suppose you can just kill me now?"

Chance answered first. "Not yet. The more dying you do, the better the outcome will be."

Dash rolled her eyes. "Chance, your bedside manner needs to be improved upon."

Ben interrupted. "Can you just knock me out? Or inject me with ketamine? I had a wonderful lucid dream the one time they gave me ketamine."

Dash placed her hand on his forehead as if to check him for fever, though it was unnecessary. "I am so sorry. You already have such a stew of chemicals in your bloodstream, we cannot take the chance of interfering with the progress of the therapy."

Chance added, "Or the chance of killing you in some unanticipated way we aren't prepared for. That could actually leave you dead."

Dash reached into a drawer. "Having said that, I do have something to help you. Quite primitive, from my days as a surgeon in remote areas of Bali, but still somewhat effective." She pulled out a leather strap and held it to his mouth. "Bite this."

Sweat broke out on Ben's brow as he bit down. He clenched his right hand; his left shook. He mumbled around the strap, "You two are the bosses."

No one spoke as Ben grimly clung to the excruciating pain of life. Finally, he passed out.

Chance leapt up. "Okay, let's get ready to revive him."

Dash rose more slowly, holding up her hand in a stop

gesture. "Not yet. We must wait." She thought about it. "We can hook up the vampire, however." They inserted the needles for the high-speed blood filtration system, the system Dash had invented originally to extract polonium from Dmitri's circulatory system.

One by one, the monitors around the room toggled to show glaring red warnings. An emergency beeper went off and Dash silenced it. Another sensor started whining, and a siren wailed, and Dash moved about the room silencing them all. Chance watched in frustration. As the last warning lights came up, Chance started pacing. "Okay, he's dead. He's really dead. The pseudo-viruses have had plenty of time to patch up his telomere chains. Time to wake him up."

Dash calmly turned on the heart and lung machine. A soft whir filled the room. She stood by the bed as her eyes roamed the monitors. "Not yet." She seemed calm, except for the way she clenched and unclenched her right hand. Eventually, she put her hand into the pocket of her lab coat. And there she stood, as Chance paced at an ever faster rate, back and forth, back and forth, while her face took on the expression of a rictus of pain not unlike Ben's just before he'd passed out.

At an obscure transition in the status reflected in the screens, Dash finally spoke. "Now!" Dash shut down the standard heart-lung machine as Chance flipped on the vampire filter. The vampire whirred ever louder as it went into high gear, flushing Ben's blood at extraordinary speed, filtering out the pseudo-viruses, and pumping the blood back into his body filled with nutrients and bursting with oxygen that should kick-start his cells and systems back into operation. Chance started the cardio massager that would periodically attempt to reactivate his heart.

More time passed; several hundred years, as far as Dash and Chance could tell. Finally, a squiggle appeared in one of the lines on the monitors and the amplified sound of a heartbeat filled the air. Both Dash and Chance slumped in exhausted relief. Chance spoke. "Let's avoid doing that again."

Dash removed her hand from her coat pocket and spread the fingers in an effort to get the kinks out. "I concur." She steadied the monitors. "It looks like we rejuvenated him for about three years." She looked down at Ben. "Not much, but enough to get him off that walker while we figure out something else."

Ben's eyes flickered open. "Two beautiful women standing over me. I guess I didn't make it. I'm in heaven."

Chance laughed, perhaps a bit too loudly. Dash once again put her hand on his forehead. "No, Ben. You are on the BrainTrust."

Ben closed his eyes, chortling. "Close enough."

Lenora looked once more at the gilt-edged invitation as she stood outside the Crystal Skull conference room. She was on the Top Men Warehouse-themed deck: the passage walls were covered in renderings of wooden crates, haphazardly stacked, stamped with labels like Top Secret and Classified, that ran in snaking lines off to infinity in all directions. Here and there the depiction of an ancient artifact marked a location in the throng of heavy boxes; she had turned left at the Ark of the Covenant to get here. She entered the conference room and was relieved to see that the skulls had been displaced from the wallscreens to make room for live video from the bottom of the ocean.

Although the room was filled with people, her attention focused on Qi Ru, who stood in front of the screens wearing a three-piece suit. He looked past Lenora at the wallscreen on the opposite side of the room, where three other men in three-piece suits were displayed, looking intently at Qi Ru and the display behind him.

That display showed a scene of bustling activity despite a mostly pitch-black background. Tiny lights like the ones on Christmas trees outlined each bot and each building, and immensely powerful spotlights illuminated a few circles on the muddy sea bottom where scattered nodules lay, waiting for collection. Based on silhouettes you could make out the nodules carried by the bots to a building where the nodules dropped into one of a clutch of baskets. An occasional bot veered off to another building to exchange batteries. A basket filled with nodules started to ascend, lifted by mylar balloons, some filled with hydrogen, others filled with oxygen. The whole system, Lenora knew, was derived from MARS, the Monterey Accelerated Research System Cabled Observatory developed decades earlier to study the sea bottom.

Lenora turned to look at the wallscreen with the three men. She recognized the conference room wherein the potential financiers sat: a room on the *GS Prime*, the isle ship built by Goldman Sachs and over half populated with Goldman Sachs employees. It was the same room where

Lenora had made her own pitch to the BrainTrust Consortium to build the Fuxing and Prometheus archipelagos.

Lenora stayed by the door and tuned into the conversation. An argument seemed to be in progress.

The financier wearing a black pinstripe suit and a brilliant gold tie complained, "Still, Qi Ru, $1.2 billion! Even our three companies together can't put up that much money. And besides, we'd like to see investment from people with a more direct stake in the project as well."

Lenora realized that while she had arrived a little late, she had arrived at a most timely moment. "Qi Ru has already invested several million dollars in bringing up the prototype operation you see here. And the BrainTrust Consortium, whom I'm authorized to represent on this archipelago, will be putting up half a billion all by themselves to build the ship where the smelting and refining of the ore will take place. So you're hardly alone."

Fleet Captain Ainsworth cleared his throat, startling Lenora with his presence. Only now did Lenora notice just how crowded the room was with people who were physically present: Jun Laquan, his parents, and Xiu Bao, all sat in a corner, clearly uncomfortable to be here. Chen Ying sat in the middle of the table, arms crossed, frowning at the financiers who were criticizing his baby. Lenora suppressed a smile at the thought of the psychological distance the Red Princeling had had to travel to think of this project, started by the imagination of a mere peasant boy, as his own.

The captain spoke, his upper-class accent once again on display. "We still need to address the elephant hiding in the corner of the room. The biggest problem with this project is the legal minefield you're about to step into."

Ainsworth shook his head grimly. "Mining the seabed is strictly regulated by a host of international laws and regulations. The Greens will scream about ecosystem damage even if the ecosystem has less life than the Sahara Desert. And all the countries of the United Nations will demand their 'fair share' of the pie. It would take longer and cost more to get the agreements into place then it would take to build the ore refining ship."

Chen Ying rolled his eyes. "How is anybody even going to know that we're doing this? Just grab the nodules off the ocean floor, bring them home, and don't tell anyone." He smiled at Lenora, offering one of her pet sayings. "Better to beg forgiveness than to ask permission."

Lenora nodded her head briefly in acknowledgment though she suspected this line of thinking would not fly with this audience. Though financiers were not technically the kind of regulatory bureaucrats to whom she typically applied such sayings, they were frequently the ones who bore the brunt of the punishment meted out by such bureaucrats. As such, they had a more cautious attitude than a college student.

Qi Ru spread his hands and spoke into the growing silence. "We could easily make billions of dollars before someone complained." He pointed to a map of the ocean floor around the archipelago with varying coloration showing the density of concentration of easily collected nodules. "Perhaps we should think of this as a short-term investment. Make a quick turnaround, pay off the cost, make a profit, and move on to something else."

Lenora tried to add encouragement. "These kinds of jurisdictional arguments are the reason we put the archipelago in this particular location in the first place, at the intersection of the boundary disputes between China, Taiwan, and the Philippines. If one of them gets angry at us, we just shift location a little and let the others dispute back."

Since she was still standing next to the door, Lenora caught a shadow of movement in the passageway. Ah, at last. "But perhaps there is another solution."

Fan Hui strode into the room, her hair shimmering as usual, drawing all eyes to her. "I hope I'm not interrupting." One corner of her lip curled as she pondered that. "Well, maybe I do hope I'm interrupting. I heard that you are discussing the startup of a mining company, and I thought I might help."

Of course she had heard about the meeting. Lenora had worked very hard to make sure she learned about it ever so indirectly.

Qi Ru responded as if he'd been expecting her. "Gentlemen, I'd like you to meet Fan Hui, daughter of the Politburo."

Lenora interrupted what promised to be a long introduction. "Fan, I'm glad you're here. We're discussing the difficulties with establishing mining rights in the ocean."

Fan Hui gave her a puzzled look. "What's difficult? These are Chinese waters for miles in all directions."

The financier with the gold tie objected. "I think the Filipinos and the Taiwanese might have a different opinion."

Fan waved the objection away derisively. "Taiwan is, of

course, a part of China, so their claims are our claims. The Filipinos have no power to object." She tilted her head sideways. "As long as we don't harm them so egregiously as to get the Americans involved, of course."

She went back to the main point. "Anyway, with me as an investor—and Chen Ying as a co-founder of course—we can easily get very good terms for the Chinese mining rights around the BrainTrust." She walked to the wallscreen and drew a red circle around the area to the south of the BrainTrust, on the Philippines side of the disputed zone. Her eyes shone as she continued. "We can get especially good terms for the rights in this part of China's territories."

Lenora coughed. "Just to be clear, Fan, we are *not* giving you a stake in the company just for your political connections."

Fan bowed her head ever so slightly in acknowledgment. "Of course not." She rolled her eyes. "You Brain-Trusters and your bizarre sense of fair play and all that." She looked at everyone around the room and on the screen. Then she looked back at Lenora. "As it happens, my dad gave me a few million renminbi to play with in case I found something fun to invest in. This is, after all, a part of the BrainTrust, and you never know when an opportunity will arise."

She looked at the prospective investors on the screen. "Would, say, fifty million renminbi be enough to acquire a stake?" She paused. "I guess I need to convert that to SmartCoin for everyone here."

The gold tie seemed uninterested in currency conversions. "No, that's fine. I'm sure we can work something out," he said with a smile. Apparently, her political backing and investment had been enough to win him over where the solid numbers and analysis of return on investment had not.

The discussion turned to the details of the financing, and Lenora lost interest except to watch proudly as her people held their own in the negotiations. Between Qi Ru's knowledge, Fan's quiet assertiveness, and Chen Ying's placid arrogance, they had the makings of a fine team.

In the end everyone shared an outline of the deal and a draft terms sheet. As the displays shut down and the team scattered, Fan pulled out her phone. "I need to call my dad, bring him up to speed since we can't really finish up this deal until we have Dad and the Politburo on board."

Lenora's time to strike had come. "Before you call your father, there's something I need to show you."

Fan paused, not quite willing to bow to Lenora's will, then put her cell away. "As you wish."

As they walked to Lenora's office, Lenora did her best to get Fan prepared for what she was about to learn. "Fan, I'd just like to make sure you clearly understand how this venture came into existence. You know, Chen Ying wasn't the primary inventor."

"Certainly not." Fan moved down the passageway with such smooth speed it was clear she was holding herself back to let Lenora keep up. "I talked with him about it. He's a software geek, not a machine junky. The peasant boy, Jun Laquan, was clearly the one who made this all possible."

Lenora nodded. "Good. I'm glad you grasp the gist of the situation." She entered her office and flipped on the wallscreen. "Normally, videotapes like this one are held in strictest confidence. But there is something so important here for you to know, I am violating my own rules."

"Really? Cool." Fan looked so eager, it was clear even a princeling was not immune to the lure of forbidden knowledge. Lenora restrained herself from mentioning that she'd actually gotten permission to show it to Fan. The air of secrecy made it ever so much more interesting.

The video started to run. Lenora restrained herself from speaking—she knew she had to let the video speak for itself.

Soon enough, Fan figured out what they were watching. "This is Jun Laquan taking the same test I did." She looked over at Lenora briefly. "The Milgram experiment. I read up about it when I told my dad about how we could use it to find traitors while they were still children."

Lenora succeeded in keeping her game face on. "Exactly."

The video ran to the end, when Jun, at the tender age of fourteen, refused the demands of the scientist. Lenora quietly shut the screen off. She turned to Fan and raised her eyebrow.

Fan pursed her lips. "So you're telling me that if we had had Milgram testing in place already, we would have executed Jun and he never would have invented the scuba bot and I wouldn't be sitting on a billion renminbi in potential profits from his efforts."

Lenora barely nodded her head. Like any teacher, Lenora felt the urge to explain further, but she knew this lesson could only be learned well enough if Fan taught it to herself. Lenora won her struggle to stay silent.

Fan continued her analysis. "You're telling me that the

characteristics of the most creative inventors and the characteristics of the most dangerous traitors are the same."

Lenora frowned.

"Of course, of course," Fan nodded her head. "It's really more complicated than that."

Lenora allowed her frown to slide away.

Fan frowned in her turn. "Honestly, I've been having restless dreams about this ever since I started working through the game theory module. The Prisoner's Dilemma, tit for tat, the iterative Prisoner's Dilemma, the mathematical foundations of both cooperation and altruism. I've been thinking that perhaps everyone in my government, even my own father, is too interested in taking and not interested enough in trading. If we traded more, there'd be more for us to take."

She sighed. "Dad was going to start the first experimental use of Milgram to execute dangerous children next week. I guess, while I'm on the phone to discuss the mining rights, I'll have to tell him to postpone the experiment indefinitely. Until I can figure it out better."

Lenora gave her a Mona Lisa smile. "You pass the test."

Now Fan looked befuddled. "The test?"

"The test to see whether you had the power of intellect to protect your own self-interest despite the disadvantages of your upbringing."

The befuddlement grew. "Disadvantages?"

Fan still looked befuddled as Lenora waved her from the room.

7

A CHANCE TO PONDER

Step 1: Use Alt-Right Recipe #1 to justify America's 35% tariff on imported goods. Step 2: use Alt-Left Recipe #1 to justify the same tariff. Extra merit tokens awarded for writeups sufficiently fantastical that they are accepted as articles by either BreitTart or Slat.

—Accel. Topic: Fake News Creation and Identification. Module: Text-based authoring of alternative facts.

Dash went to the cafeteria a bit early, though she did not pick up a tray or get any food. She searched the tables for the target of her coming interrogation.

A middle-aged woman with white hair wearing a business suit rose from a small table: Amanda, her boss of sorts, and the current Chairman of the Board for the BrainTrust Consortium. Meanwhile, still seated at the table was the man she sought.

Dash hurried over. "*Bu* Amanda," she said with a slight bow. "It is good to see you."

Colin started to rise, but Dash waved him back to his seat. "*Pak* Colin, please, I need to ask you a question."

Amanda chuckled. "Oh, we all need to ask him questions. But will he answer any of the questions we really need answered? Will he even tell us what the right questions are?" With that, she waved goodbye and strode off.

Dash sat opposite Colin. He gave her an innocent smile. "How can I help you?"

"I wish to know if you hired Chance to replace me in the event I was captured or killed in one of these kidnapping attempts."

Colin looked at her wide-eyed.

"My first intern, Byron, had a very different skill set from me. I knew far more about molecular biology than he, and he knew far more about software engineering than I. We were quite complementary. And we were able to make progress at a remarkable rate working together." She pressed her lips together for a moment. "Chance, on the other hand, has a skill set very similar to mine. Such redundancy seems less efficient, but it reduces risk if you are afraid of losing me."

Colin closed his eyes. Dash was pretty sure he was rolling his eyes to heaven underneath the lids. He sighed. "First of all, as you and I have discussed before, it is possible for one design to have more than one purpose. So I suppose it is true enough that choosing Chance for your intern reduces the risk that your research will fail if the Chief Advisor or the Premier or someone else succeeds. But that's far from the most important reason."

He stared directly into her eyes. "Dash, where do the critical problems lie in the development of your telomere therapy? Do they lie in the development of the software? Or in the development of the machinery driven by the software? If either of these were the case, then another intern like Byron would make sense. But if the critical trouble lies in the molecular biology or the biochemistry, would it not make sense to have a second person with skills similar to your own, with whom you could bounce ideas back and forth?"

Dash sat back in her chair as she contemplated this alternate interpretation. "You are right, *Pak* Colin. Looking back, I see that we have, indeed, actually collaborated on improvements to the therapy itself."

Colin smiled. "Excellent." He pursed his lips. "Now, in the spirit of full disclosure, let me add another reason why I thought you should have another person with skills similar to your own. Chance does enable your telomere research to continue even if we lose you."

Dash pointed a finger at him. "I knew it. You are preparing a backup plan in the face of these kidnappers."

Colin looked to the sky and laughed. "No that's not where I was going." He looked back at her with amusement. "Tell me, Dash, what are some of the things you would like to work on besides telomeres? Clearly, you like working on the molten salt nuclear reactors. And it looks like you're having a delightful time with Matt's rocketry. Anything else?"

Dash looked away pensively. "Well, I have some odd thoughts on how Ted could improve the range of his copters. And there's another kind of nuclear reactor, quite different from molten salt, that might be useful for small-scale applications. I've been talking to Rhett about it." She paused for a moment letting her head shake from side to side. "And there is this problem with current conceptions of punctuated equilibrium evolutionary theory that no one else seems to have noticed. I should really talk to somebody about it." Her eyes lit up. "And--"

Colin held his hands up in surrender. "Okay, enough already!" He put his hands down. "Don't you see? With Chance there to take over many of the responsibilities in your primary research, you have more time to work with other people on other things. We're not going to lose you to kidnappers, Dash. But your telomere research could easily lose part of you to other important projects."

As she thought about it, Dash's eyes gleamed. "Thank you, *Pak* Colin. I had not thought of that at all." She blew out a breath. "I have been feeling so guilty about my work with Matt on the new rockets. You have made me feel… relieved." Her whole body seemed to relax.

Colin reached out and gingerly touched her hand. "Making people's lives easier is just what we do." He chuckled. "Well, making *some* people's lives easier." He sat back in his chair. "Now, as it happens I have had, for many years, an itch I have been unable to scratch. The itch has been getting worse ever since Alex solved one of my problems by building that two-deck-high 3D printer SpaceR uses to manufacture one-piece rocket boosters. The only thing left that I still need to scratch my itch is a smaller power supply. What have you got?"

Dash switched thought modes with easy speed. "It's not really a reactor, it's a battery. I too have had an itch I could not scratch, ever since I helped design the new reef for Matt. We wound up using solar panels because our standard reactors are just too…"

"Overkill. For that application they're overpowered, expensive to build, and despite the simplifications in the design, a considerable amount of logistical effort to maintain."

"Just so." Dash turned pensive. "For long-range space probes that travel too far for solar power, they use Plutonium-238, the isotope that does *not* produce fission, to generate heat that they convert into electricity using thermocouples. The efficiency is too low to be satisfactory, but worse, Pu-238 is very difficult to produce. There are less than fifty kilograms in the whole world at this time."

Colin nodded to show he was paying attention. "And the solution?"

"Strontium-90, with either a Stirling engine or direct betavoltaic conversion to electricity. Sr-90 produces only beta radiation, if we can collect the beta electrons directly, it can be very efficient indeed. And if we can capture the electrons without generating bremsstrahlung gamma rays, we can keep the shielding surprisingly thin and light."

"How difficult is it to get the Sr-90?"

Dash smiled. "Easy. We already produce Sr-90 in our reactors. They are tuned to keep the Sr-90 in the reactor and burn it since it's quite dangerous if emitted into the environment, but we can re-tune the systems to extract it for us. So how much power do you need?"

"Maybe a hundred kilowatts."

"Hmmm… Do you have a good heatsink?"

Colin chuckled. "Oh, yes, believe me, the heat sink for this application is excellent."

Dash nodded as she did some computations in her head. "Then we can use the Stirling engine if I cannot make the betavoltaic conversion work. I think we can make the whole system about half a ton in weight. Too much?"

Colin put his hands together. "That should be fine." He leaned forward again. "I think I can talk Amanda into giving this a priority. I'll talk with her, you talk with Rhett. Sooner rather than later?"

"Sooner rather than later," Dash promised. Her eyes gleamed. "I see now why you gave me Chance."

Colin had barely stepped away from the table when Chance herself plunked her tray down next to Dash. Chance eyed Colin as he moved toward the dish recycling station. "That's Colin Wheeler, right? I've heard a lot about him. He seems really important, but no one can explain to me exactly how or why he's important. I tried looking him up in the archipelago directory. He doesn't have an entry. I thought everybody had an entry. Who is he, really?"

Dash opened her mouth, then closed it. How to explain *Pak* Colin? She thought about how he had turned the enemies of the BrainTrust against each other. Did that make him a symphony conductor, or choreographer? And she thought about how he had just now relieved her of the guilt from following too many projects at once. Did that make him the embodiment on earth of the Hindu God Ganesha, the Remover of Obstacles? And she thought about how he had stepped in front of her as Byron had started shooting. What did that make him? It was too much. She gave the best answer she could in a few words. "He is indeed a very important person. He is a friend."

One of the nice things about Chance was that she understood the depth of that answer, and accepted it as complete.

Ping stood on the top deck of the *Mount Parnassus* with Ciara, watching the isle ships maneuver into their archipelago positions off the west coast of Africa.

Ciara sighed with relief. "It's about time. This was a wicked long journey."

Ping concurred. "Too long with the Fuxing, building them another manufacturing ship. Really, I need to give Colin and Matt a piece of my mind, holding us up like that."

Ciara eyed her shrewdly. "You didn't complain one bit till Jam left. And then you still got to clock Guang Jian for her."

"Yeah, well..." Ping pointed into the distance. "Is that a welcoming committee?"

Ciara looked in the direction Ping pointed. "Not necessarily. We haven't advertised our arrival yet, didn't want any enthusiasts rushing out to us before we were ready. Things could've gotten ugly with those half-drowned sampans when the Fuxing first arrived on station, I thought we'd wanna avoid that." She continued to peer at the ship that seemed to be approaching them. "Of course, it could be a different kind of welcoming committee. We're parking much closer to the land here, barely twelve miles off the coast of Benin, only a little farther from Nigeria. Piracy is rife around here. We didn't want anyone who was trying to reach us to get hijacked before we could help them."

Ping's smile widened into an expression of glee. "Hot damn! I think it's a warship of some kind. I don't think they like us being here."

Ciara looked thoughtful. "Benin does have a couple of old French patrol boats for anti-piracy operations. But since the port at Cotonou flooded, along with half the coastal areas, and a bunch of ex-Boko Haram fanatics took control of the government, the Benin government itself has operated the most successful pirate fleet in the area." She thought about it some more. "It may have been a mistake setting up the Prometheus archipelago this close to the coast."

Ping whooped. "Are you kidding me? You were right the first time—if we set up further out, the pirates would be snagging everyone who wants to join the BrainTrust. We have to be here." She pulled out her cell phone. "Hey, Soup! I need the Big Gun! Make it snappy!" She called the Fleet Captain next. "Captain! Can you see what kind of gun that is on the front of the patrol boat approaching us? A 50mm? Thanks!"

She turned away from Ciara. "Can't sit here waiting for them, that gun has better range than we've got. Hafta go out to meet them. Gotta get together with Soup on the copter pad in back." She cackled as she departed.

Soup flew the copter while Ping hung out the passenger door, trying to get an angle where the Big Gun's backblast wouldn't burn Soup to a crisp. "Soup, take us higher, give me more deflection!"

Down below the crew of the patrol ship was shouting, trying to point the gun at the copter. They popped off a couple rounds, shot some AK-47s in the air, all to no avail. Disregarding the copter at last, they turned their sights on the isle ships of the Prometheus fleet. They fired, but the shot landed far short and off to the side.

Ping was finally happy with the angle. "Ok, Soup, hold her here." The Big Gun hummed to life, targeting the enemy ship. "I've got you now!" Ping exclaimed as she prepared to press the trigger.

Suddenly a flash of uncontrolled fire erupted from the stern of the patrol ship. Black smoke then belched forth, obscuring the flames. The ship slowed and drifted to starboard as if the rudder had twisted.

Ping stared in exasperation. "Are you kidding me? I didn't even get a shot in!" She glanced at the Prometheus ships. "Did someone else shoot before I got the chance? But they're too far away."

Soup sympathized with her. "Doesn't look like the ship's been very well maintained. In fact, not maintained at all." He flew lower. "Look at all the rust on that bucket."

Ping groaned. "Now we'll have to rescue them. And we can't send them back to Benin, they'll just start pirating again. So what're we going to do for a prison? Make the ship they're on into a prison?"

Soup headed the copter for home. "Quite a mess, winning a battle like that."

Dmitri strolled along the outside walkway of the *Dreams*, taking in the crisp evening air, just approaching the gangway to the *Haven*, to his home. He spread his arms wide as if trying to grasp the entire world. He still felt amazed to be alive, even more amazed to still be wealthy, and most amazed of all to still be a member of the Brain-Trust. He strove now to be indispensable for the Brain-Trusters. His investments covered the gamut of projects on the archipelago. He never would have predicted things could work out this well, given the circumstances he'd found himself in when he first brought his yacht alongside the Elysian Fields.

"Dmitri!" he heard his name called. He turned to see Colin Wheeler jogging toward him.

Dmitri watched him approach, puzzled, but smiling nonetheless. "How can I help you?"

Colin shook his head, "I'm good. Believe it or not, sometimes I don't come asking favors. Sometimes I even offer them." He held out a small cardboard box. "A memento."

Dmitri mechanically accepted the proffered gift. "Thank you, I guess."

Colin laughed and slapped him on the shoulder. "You should definitely look this gift horse in the mouth. But don't worry. As long as you're careful with it, it won't harm you." And with that Colin jogged cheerily away.

Dmitri took the box up to his dwelling, nodding to Gina as she went out. Gina seemed to have forgiven him, at least sort of, despite her first whispered words to him after his release: *"Kidnap anyone again, and I'll strap you to a rocket engine test stand. Ever seen a steak after being broiled by five million pounds of thrust? I have. That's you."*

It had occurred to him that the threat was neither idle nor impractical—not at least for Gina—but it didn't bother him. He believed in loyalty and honor, and he had no intention of doing anything disloyal or dishonorable to the people of the BrainTrust again.

Reaching his desk, he picked up his old Smersh-5 combat knife and sliced the seal on the box. Inside was a dull gray lead vial, diligently sealed, and a simple manila envelope.

He stared at the vial, then picked up the envelope. He used his index finger to reach under the flap and tear it open.

The letter inside the envelope was short.

Dmitri,

Over the years, I have been drawn to the conclusion that we should always keep mementos of our most striking near-death experiences. To keep us appreciative of our second chances, to keep us alert.

We extracted this from your blood. Rhett Woodson on the Chiron can dispose of it for you if you'd prefer. Or you can keep it if you have a safe enough place for it. Your choice.

Dmitri stared again at the vial of polonium. If he had any sense, he would take it directly to Rhett. But... he wasn't sure what he wanted to do with it. So, until he figured it out, he decided to put it in the wall vault behind the bookcase next to his desk. Not only was the vault almost impossible to find, the vault manufacturer guaranteed it against just about everything short of a tactical nuke. The vial should be safe enough there.

For generations, the California coastal housing market had boomed. Decade after decade, ever since they had first started bulldozing the orange groves to make way for office complexes, the value of real estate had risen on an exponential curve faster than the median income of those desiring a place to call home. Prices became obscene. Wise men asserted they had to go down, and a small dip in prices heralded loud claims that the end was finally nigh. But as real estate markets across America crashed and burned and were reborn weaker and smaller, California real estate continued to ride the wave of human hope and determination. Even after Deportation Phase II had driven all the foreign engineers out of Silicon Valley and obliterated the workforce to collect the almonds, oranges, and avocados from the remaining fields, coastal California real estate had dipped but then recovered as miraculously as a phoenix.

It was too good to be true. And like most things too good to be true, it was not true, though it took truth almost a century to emerge.

Truth made its first stumbling appearance on the California scene after the news broke that the entire SpaceR operations, manufacturing, and launch systems had moved to the BrainTrust. Truth thumped its first victims when the excessively wealthy learned that Gina Toscano had sold her mansion without pursuing an upgrade to an even bigger mansion.

Truth started a rout of its opponents after the Cogent News article published its list of all the people targeted for civil forfeiture proceedings.

It takes surprisingly little truth to topple a grossly over-priced and overleveraged real estate market. When the billionaires all put their mansions on the market at the same time, the millionaires noticed that they could upgrade at very reasonable prices. Prices that fell quickly to mirror the prices of the smaller mansions of the million-aires. The millionaires moved swiftly to trade up...but only the first few made the trade before the values of the smaller mansions started falling. Soon the upper middle class started demanding millionaire mansions for a middle-class price and the values of middle-class homes fell, to be met with a shocking lack of buyers even at the new lower prices since so many middle-class people learned their companies were moving out of the state and leaving them behind.

The California government, as dependent on real estate taxes as it was on corporate taxes that were also disappear-ing, found its traditional, steady, reliable revenues plum-meting towards the bottom of a pit as impervious to human preferences as the concrete launch pad of a rocket booster.

8

SIBERIA

I don't make jokes. I just watch the government and report the facts.
    —Will Rogers

Jam struggled in vain to keep an eye on Julissa and her copter as she slipped her own copter low and fast through the midnight darkness over the border from Northern China into Russia. "Important safety tip," Jam muttered to herself, "it's very hard to keep track of a stealth copter if you want to make sure it's following you." She resisted the urge to call Julissa and tell her to shut off the stealth mode. Either the Russians or the Chinese or both would nail them in minutes without it.

Had the copter actually needed her piloting skills, she undoubtedly would have died already; she was simply not paying enough attention. In the end, she gave up her attempts to find Julissa and turned forward to watch the snowcapped trees glow in the moonlight. She had to put her faith in the GPS systems aboard both copters to land them in the same place.

Absurd side trips seemed to be the hallmark of life as an Expedition Commander. She reflected on her phone call to Dash after she had gotten familiar with the copters as Dash had requested:

Dash explained, and Jam tried to object. "You want me to go where? You want me to do what?" Jam pulled out her tablet and looked at the map. "Do you have any idea how deep in Siberia that is?" She listened further. "Ok, I get it, we've got to get his wife and daughter so Joshua can let Gleb out of the brig. But... whoa, they may be guarded by Alexei and Vasily? The same two who...oh no, certainly not a problem, just wish Ping were here, she'll be upset to be left out...ok, just for you."

Jam had hung up shaking her head.

Now she was deep in Siberia in search of the family of a former kidnapper and attempted murderer. Life with the BrainTrust truly had its own flavor and tempo.

Eventually, Jam reached the specified coordinates and the autopilot brought the copter down behind an embankment of snow separated from the rutted road by a couple rows of evergreens. Moments later a shadow occluded the moon, and Julissa landed behind her. Jam trudged back to her partner in crime.

Julissa's eyes gleamed. "This is *so* exciting," she whispered.

Jam grunted. "Just stay here with the copters. If someone finds you and stops to investigate, at the first hint of trouble, take your copter home."

"You're really sure you don't want me to come along? I could carry a gun if you wanted me to."

Jam rolled her eyes. Julissa had lived an impoverished life, not only in terms of wealth but also in terms of experiences. She was enjoying this little excursion—breaking and entering into the territory of a superpower—entirely too much. Jam hissed, "Stay here."

With those parting words, Jam picked her way through the trees onto the road and followed her GPS to the destination not quite a kilometer away. The sky brightened within moments of reaching the road. Her timing had been entirely too close, they had landed the copters barely in time to avoid being visible in daylight.

Vasily stood in the snow outside the dacha and rubbed his eye to clear that hazy film blurring his vision. He couldn't help rubbing it. Fiddling with the eye was instinctual; it made no difference knowing there was no film on it. No clearing of the blur was possible; his electronic replacement eye saw things as well as it could. Dash had told him it was remarkably good, all things considered.

He watched the little girl run through the snow, laughing as she shaped snowballs to throw at her mom. He observed to himself that he had had much less pleasant postings than this, watching over Gleb's wife and child in the middle of a wasteland so vast it served as a prison all by itself. The only place you could go within five kilometers to find another human being was the real prison, an actual godforsaken gulag. The gulag served as a constant reminder that his life could be so much worse.

And of course just outside the gulag was a cemetery to remind one that even the gulag could look good compared to other alternatives. Yet he still wanted to avoid the gulag.

This thought brought him around to watch Alexei scowling at the two women. Alexei had assumed that part of the job should be using the woman and the child for his personal pleasure. After all, Gleb had failed in his mission and deserved punishment.

Alexei's assumptions did not fit with Vasily's own interpretation of the Premier's curt instructions. "Hold them. Keep them unharmed, and hold them." He could easily imagine winding up in the gulag because of the Premier's differing opinion on the meaning of the word "unharmed."

On the other hand, he could also easily imagine winding up in the cemetery because of Alexei's fierce defense of his own interpretation of the word. Keeping Alexei from running amuck was a constant dangerous balancing act.

Life had been so much simpler and better on the BrainTrust.

A melodious female voice, muffled by the snow but nonetheless strong and clear, came from behind a tree very close at hand. "Let me see your hands," the voice said in English with a distinct British accent. "Move and die."

Vasily finally placed the voice. He had heard it during Ben Wilson's First Launch party that now seemed to have occurred thousands of years ago. Jam, as he recalled, had explained she had learned English from the Brits as a Pakistani commando.

Vasily started to raise his hands, but the little girl ran in front of Alexei, who grabbed her as she passed and pressed his gun to her head.

Alexei hissed, "Grab the wench, or I'll shoot you myself."

Gleb's wife stood, confused, near at hand. Vasily grabbed her and matched Alexei's pose. He whispered urgently to Alexei, "Throw the gun down, you idiot, or she'll drop us where we stand."

Alexei shouted at the tree, "Come out with your hands up, or the girl dies."

Vasily rolled his eyes. This was going to go so badly so quickly.

Jam swore under her breath. She'd been watching them for some time, making sure there were no other soldiers around, trying to decide whether to just shoot the two men or give them a chance to live. In the end, she had screwed up. Correcting the error was going to be complicated.

Jam shifted her gun to her left hand, raised both her hands, and stepped out from behind the tree.

Alexei smiled. "Oh, things are going to be so much better now. At last, someone to play with." He took a deeper breath, and shouted to Jam, "Drop the gun!"

Vasily called, "Alexei, you can't play with her, she's a *BrainTrust commando!*"

This acknowledgment stopped Jam cold for a moment. At last someone respected her skills! About time. Unfortunate circumstances, however.

Jam spoke calmly to Alexei. "Very well, dropping the gun now." She watched him for a moment, confirming that he had started to relax, and had shifted his gun to point at her rather than the girl.

Jam released the gun from her left hand. It fell.

Then Jam let her knees fold. As she fell, and the gun fell, she swept up the gun with her right hand.

Alexei fired. He had aimed at her chest while she was standing; the bullet barely creased her shoulder. Jam fired back and rolled sideways.

Alexei fell like a stone, which indeed he was. With his medulla oblongata now turned to pureed soup, his body fell without so much as a finger twitch.

Jam rolled to her knees, expecting at any moment to be struck by a shot from Vasily.

He couldn't miss, not with his Spetsnaz training. Her only real chance was to take the bullet and kill him while she bled out. Julissa could then get Gleb's family home.

So, with more determination than hope, Jam sighted her gun on the limited part of her target not blocked by the mother. If he just held off shooting for another moment...

Then Vasily jerked his arm and tossed his gun into the snow. He raised his hands and slid to his knees, mimicking her. "Jam. Please. Take me with you."

Jam almost lowered her weapon in surprise, but then she remembered who she was dealing with—one of Dash's kidnappers. She held the gun steady on his chest.

The woman spoke. "Please don't hurt him. He's been protecting us."

Jam knelt speechless for a moment. Not only was the victim defending him, but it dawned on her that if she left him behind, the Premier would vent his wrath on his failed guard. If Jam didn't take him along, he would end up in the gulag's cemetery.

In the end, there was only one thing for Jam to say. "Ok."

After zip-tying Vasily, Jam led them all back to the copters where the real problem awaited her. She was about to play the old game of carrying a chicken, a fox, and a basket of corn across the river. Unfortunately, her boat was even smaller than the boat used in the game. She addressed the mother. "Tatiana, can you fly a copter?"

Tatiana shook her head.

Jam persisted. "How about your daughter?"

Tatiana snapped at her. "You are *not* going to make my daughter a copter pilot." She reflected. "Well, not today. She has no idea."

Vasily offered, "I know how to fly a copter."

Of course he did. Well, it would have to do. She sliced the zip ties from his hands. "Disobey my orders, and I'll find you and gut you."

He rubbed his wrists. "I wouldn't have it any other way."

Jam stepped back and spoke to her companions. "Okay, those of you who are numerically gifted will have noticed that we have two copters, each able to carry two people, and five people. Julissa, you'll fly the copter with Misha. Vasily, you'll fly the copter with Tatiana."

Julissa beat the others to the punch in asking the obvious question. "But what about you?"

Jam took a deep breath. "Don't worry about me. I've made my way across more hostile terrain than this. The last time I had nothing but the clothes on my back." She forced a cheery note into her voice. "This time, I'm much better equipped." She looked to the south, across the bleakness that went on forever.

Vasily coughed. "I don't think even I could make it across that countryside, and I can at least blend in as a Russian."

Jam jerked her head up and down. "Which is why I'll be the one who goes on foot." She wiggled the gun pointed at him. "Don't make me tell you again."

Vasily raised his hands. "Whatever you say, boss."

As they lifted off, Jam wrapped her coat tighter around herself, pulled her scarf low, and headed south.

As the meeting on liftoff schedules broke up, Matt saw Dash standing humbly outside the conference room. He waved her in. "Dash. Good to see you. What can I do for you?"

Werner had risen to leave, but when he saw Dash, he stopped. "Hey, how's it going?"

Dash entered the room smiling. "My main research continues to make progress. And I think we've made some progress on your request as well."

Matt looked back and forth between the two conspirators. "Werner, what request is that?"

Werner blushed. "I've been meaning to tell you. I asked Dash to look into making the *Heinlein*-class ships faster. Like all the isle ships, the *Heinlein* at full thrust makes about four knots. It would be great if our ships could move faster."

Dash added, "you're not the only ones who want faster ships. Of course, the most basic requirement of an isle ship, namely stability while stationary in high seas, is in conflict with the needs of speed. Even though the ships have plenty of power for more propellers, fluid resistance grows as a cube of speed. Trying to just push harder through the water would create large waves but little speed. To go faster, you simply must achieve better streamlining." She synced the wallscreen to her tablet. "Fortunately there is a solution."

On the screen they could see the outline of a standard isle ship, with its barge-like prow and the two reactor modules underneath. "Alex's folks from the *Argus* who figured out how to grow isle ship hulls the way clams grow seashells have been studying ice."

Matt blinked. "Ice?"

Dash covered her mouth to prevent a giggle. "I didn't expect it either."

She started an animation on the display. Copper-colored lines formed a frame from the bow to the stern, caging the nuclear pods in a shape that looked like a traditional ship hull. "They were trying to grow a temporary hull out of ice using a copper wire frame, but the wiring was too stiff for setup and disassembly, it tended to break. We equipped the Prometheus fleet with it anyway, they had such a long way to go. It helped them tremendously, but it just wasn't practical for widespread application."

Now most of the copper lines were replaced by black lines that waved slightly in the current though they were anchored to the remaining copper lines. "Then I introduced Alex's team to the fellows on the *Dreams* who made the Graphene Reinforced Carbon tiles for your launch pads."

Matt nodded; GRC was the first invention Dash had introduced him to.

"One of the reasons graphene works so well for the tiles is that it is an incredible heat conductor. So incredible that they had to modify Fourier's Law of heat transfer to explain it." Now the copper disappeared completely from the animation, replaced by thicker black lines. "We figured out how to make a folding skeleton of graphene that could create an ice hull in hours rather than days. The ice hull is highly streamlined. And since ice floats, it actually lifts the ship itself out of the water. Only the highly streamlined shape of the ice remains. The Prometheus experiment suggests we might get fifteen or sixteen knots, a factor of four."

Werner leaned forward eagerly. "How soon can I get it?"

Matt corrected the question. "How soon can we get it without paying a rush order premium?"

Dash laughed gaily. "We can put the *Heinlein* second on the list. First will be the *Haven* since they're willing to pay a premium."

Werner headed to the door. "Good enough. Thank you again, Dash."

Matt waited until Werner had departed before looking at Dash. "Ice hulls are not the reason you're here, is it?"

Dash sat down next to Matt and placed her tablet before him for a more intimate presentation. "No. I need urgently to speak with you about cell phone satellites."

Matt looked at Dash curiously. "Cell phone satellites? What does that even mean?"

Dash brought up a new animation on her tablet, of a chunk of Earth with satellites zooming at various altitudes above it. "You already have a fleet of broadband satellites, StarLink."

Matt nodded. "My predecessor built it quite a while ago. It was never as profitable as we'd hoped—too much competition. By the time we had ours full up, three other companies were well on their way to completing theirs."

Dash raised an eyebrow. "Was that the only problem?"

He added reluctantly, "And too much equipment needed on the ground." He held his hands out to outline an object the shape of a pizza box. "Even though the ground relay was small and cheap by Western standards, it was a considerable hurdle for most potential users."

Dash highlighted a StarLink satellite on the tablet, then highlighted a satellite in a much lower orbit.

"This is the proposed Starry Night cell phone satellite. Think of it as a cell tower in the sky."

Matt studied the screen. "So your cell phone could hook directly into the satellite? No ground station at all?"

"Exactly."

Matt shook his head. "There are so many problems with this I don't know where to begin." He swept his finger up and down from the Starry Night to the earth and back. "You need really low latency for a cell phone."

Dash nodded. "And that's a really low orbit satellite. Much closer than StarLink."

Matt frowned. "Which means it's so low that atmospheric friction is bound to be a problem."

Dash fingered the tablet and blew up the image of the satellite into a schematic diagram. "Which is why it has ion propulsion jets working continuously, and a set of chemical propellant thrusters for periodic high-G corrections."

Matt whistled. "Those are big fuel tanks for the thrusters."

Dash shrugged. "Colin muttered something about needing to be able to dodge space junk as it reentered atmosphere." She paused. "Professor Dillion and I both thought the tanks could be smaller, but Colin was adamant."

So Colin was involved. Interesting. "Power?"

"Strontium-90 batteries."

Matt had no idea what that meant, but Dash was so confident, he let it go. Finally, he got to the core problem. "It looks fabulous, Dash, but I don't have the money for a project this large. Not anymore. My R&D fund has been pretty well depleted."

Dash gave him a big grin. She pulled out her cell. "Ben, Colin, Keenan, you can come in now."

Matt ran his tongue over his teeth. "Sounds like you have a plan for the financing as well. You are the complete hand, Dr. Dash."

Dash covered her mouth with her hand. "I will take that as a compliment, even if it is not."

Matt wasn't sure himself whether it was a compliment or not, so he said nothing.

When Colin, Ben, and Keenan arrived, a round of comfortable haggling began. Matt was determined to force his investors to take a full forty-nine percent stake. Colin, on behalf of the BrainTrust, offered a thirty-five/sixty-five percent split. Ben wanted a piece and insisted Dash take a tiny slice as well. She had the money, he explained, and she needed good investments.

Dash easily agreed, on one condition. "Before we put all the money in, we need to do some experimenting. As it happens, Professor Dillion and his grad students have a prototype of the Starry Night satellite. We should launch it immediately, and see how it performs."

Werner, who had been recalled to the room for scheduling and technical assessment, concurred. "Absolutely! We won't know the real cost until we have the real satellite in our hands and some experience with maintaining and refueling the damn things."

Everyone agreed to these terms and went back to haggling.

While Colin and Ben argued over the split of the forty-five percent Matt had compromised with them on, Matt negotiated with Keenan on financing the half of SpaceR's fifty-five percent that couldn't come out of his R&D budget. Matt and Werner kept looking at their current cash flow, which had improved significantly since moving to the BrainTrust, to see how much they could fund out of future profits.

Dash showed Matt her calculations on how profitable it would be to bring direct cell phone connections to every person on earth, bypassing government monopolies and taxation policies: with a direct satellite connection, the governments wouldn't even know there were phone calls to be taxed.

The profit numbers were huge, so huge Dash apologized at one point. "I know this sounds like a ridiculously large amount of profit, but I cannot find anything wrong with my calculations. I keep trying to find a reason to make the numbers small enough to be believable, but I cannot."

Matt kept pondering those numbers. He couldn't see anything wrong with them either. It would be very profitable. He needed more.

In the end, Matt negotiated his investors into taking only a thirty-three percent stake. Goldman Sachs offered SpaceR a line of credit for anything they couldn't pay for out of current savings and future profits.

As people departed, Matt muttered, "Did I just out-negotiate everybody in the room, or did I just hang myself?"

Colin slapped him on the shoulder. "If I knew, I wouldn't tell you."

Dash yelled at Werner. "I want to get that prototype up as soon as possible. Any way we could launch it tomorrow?"

Werner stared at her. "What's the rush?"

Dash smiled mischievously. "I need to make a phone call."

On the way into his home office, the Premier passed one of his general-purpose bots on the way out. That was a little unusual, though not so unusual as to set off any alarm bells. In the Russian Union as in so much of the civilized world, GP bots were illegal...but of course, he'd made an exception for himself. The things were quite useful, and his human staff tasked the bots as often as he did. And he preferred the bot to his human staff for coming and going from his office: it felt more private.

Reaching his desk, the Premier discovered a small cardboard box sitting dead-center on top of the closed lid of his laptop. He stared at it for a moment, saw in tiny writing in the upper left corner a sender address of sorts: "The Brain-Trust." It was addressed to "The Premier."

Surely his security detail had examined it already. But if it was really from the BrainTrust perhaps not, perhaps the BrainTrust had circumvented...well, if it were from the BrainTrust it would be harmless, of that at least he felt confident.

The BrainTrust continued to irritate him in numerous ways. He found himself daydreaming more and more often about how much less problematic all those half-baked geniuses would be if just a few key people mysteriously died. But he had a rule: don't kill someone unless he woke up dreaming about their deaths every morning for two weeks in a row. His BrainTrust death dreams had only started eight days ago.

He ripped at the tape on the box. It opened easily. Inside he found a dull gray lead vial, diligently sealed. The Premiere felt a chill run down his spine.

A blank manila envelope accompanied the vial. He reached under the flap with his index finger to tear it open.

Ouch! The edge of the flap sliced his finger. He stared at the thin red line. He supposed he couldn't really blame the BrainTrust for his clumsiness. Of course, he was the Premier. Perhaps he could blame them anyway.

The letter inside the envelope contained nothing but a page of gibberish: random letters, lowercase and uppercase and numeric and alphabetic. Cyphertext.

Would he have to drag his best decryption experts all the way out here from their Cozy Bear headquarters in Red Square?

Another chill went down his spine as he became convinced he knew the decryption key. At least, his computer knew the decryption key—the super-key used to breach all the computer chips not made on the BrainTrust.

He scanned the letter into the laptop and set his software to transcribing it. Sure enough, out came the cleartext, demonstrating that that bastard knew he had the super-key.

Premier,

I have been terribly remiss and tardy in sending you a congratulatory note on your new title. I thought the occasion deserved an appropriate inauguration gift.

As you may have guessed, the vial contains polonium. One of your people seems to have misplaced it on the BrainTrust. We thought you might like to return it to an appropriately secure holding facility.

Forgive me, but as a member of the BrainTrust, we are always seeking new markets and new opportunities. As you may know, we too have the ability to manufacture polonium. If you find yourself running short, we would be happy to sell you more at a price I think you will find attractive.

We can deliver it in raw form, as we have presented it here, but we can also deliver it prepackaged in hypodermic syringes, in metal tips for walking canes, and of course on the edges of manila envelopes for convenient delivery.

How should we deliver it to you?

No signature accompanied the missive. Unnecessary. Only one person would send a package like this.

Sweat burst out on the Premier's forehead. He looked at the thin line of blood welling on his finger. Death came so easily disguised. He forced himself to take a deep breath, to calm himself. He was confident there had been no polonium on the envelope. This had merely been a warning. But he would now have to rush to the hospital just to make sure.

Not that his doctors could do anything if he had been poisoned. The only person who had a cure was thousands of miles away, and she had good reasons to cheer his poisoning along. It was all damnably irritating.

How the hell had that bastard delivered it *to his private office?*

The GP bot had of course brought the box the last few

steps. The BrainTrust had of course manufactured the bot. All GP bots came from the archipelago. Could they have put a backdoor into all *their* chips, and used that to subvert the bot?

No, no, their reputation was too precious to them. That bastard would not do something so obvious and harmful to the archipelago's long-run interests. Surely he had simply exploited human fallibility: the deliveryman thinks the box is high priority, he gives it to a new employee who hasn't yet fully internalized the importance of the security team's inclusion in the mail protocol, he hurriedly gives it to the bot...and voila, a simple loophole in the man/machine interface opens up.

Another aspect of this still nagged at him. Ah, yes, the encrypted letter. Did that bastard also have the decryption super-key? Could he read and subvert all the computers in the world the way the Premier himself and the Chief Advisor could? If the Premier remembered his limited encryption knowledge correctly, it was easy to encrypt such messages without the decryption key.

Besides, how could the BrainTrust acquire five of the seven keys needed to build the super-key? Bribery and blackmail seemed outside the domain of their prissy morality.

Then the Premier had a terrible realization. That bastard could have gotten the super-key from the Premier himself.

It was obvious in retrospect. That bastard would let the Premier do the heavy lifting of constructing the super-key and putting the whole thing on his own laptop. Then the

BrainTrust would use a technique not unlike the one used just now to deliver the polonium, only this time install a virus on the laptop rather than leaving a box on the lid. One stop shopping for the geeks of the BrainTrust.

He still wasn't certain Colin had the key. But he had to assume so. For a wild moment, he considered getting all the computers in the Russian government and military upgraded with BrainTrust chips to lock those bastards out. But that would deprive not only Colin but also himself of the ubiquitous spying capability so necessary to the maintenance of his rule.

Calming down, the Premier realized that maintaining total information awareness for himself was so important he had to tolerate the BrainTrust's ownership of the same power.

He was quite sure now that he would continue to wake up with dreams about dealing decisively with the BrainTrust. But he was also quite sure that, even after a month of such dreams, he would take no action.

***

The governor stood outside the briefing room, waiting for the place to fill with reporters, controlling his urge to cheer. These were exciting times. California had not started a new welfare program for over a decade. He would now achieve a goal that had eluded his predecessor for his entire career.

A lot of billionaires had escaped the forfeiture proceedings, but enough had not. Not only had the resulting windfall balanced the state's budget, but it had also actually created the first surplus in the governor's lifetime.

He had initially planned to put the surplus into a rainy day fund. But when the California legislature found out they had money to spare, they moved swiftly to seize the opportunity. Sure, the windfall was a one-time-only affair. Yes, revenues from both business taxes and real estate taxes were collapsing.

But the people in the legislature were politicians. They knew surely, as surely as an astronomer knows the sun will rise, that the businesses would return and the real estate market would rise—because they always had in the past.

And the politicians necessarily believed that once a new level of revenue had been achieved, that somehow that much revenue would continue to flow in all future years, no matter how murky the mechanism for such a flow might be. Windfall or not, this was the only chance they were ever likely to have to start a new program.

In the next few minutes the governor would make the announcement that the Affordable Child, Worker, and Consumer Protection Program would kick off immediately.

But even the ACWCPP was not the big news. The Attorney General had found a wondrous silver lining in the departure of the billionaires.

The AG had revealed his insight during a discussion of the civil forfeiture cases being prepared. The governor remembered it clearly.

The AG had started with the bad news. "You probably won't be surprised to hear that a number of companies are moving their operations to Red states, the disloyal bastards."

The governor had shrugged. In retrospect, he could see that this was inevitable fallout from the SpaceR debacle. "What about their billionaire owners?"

The AG growled. "Even the ones who're leaving their businesses in California are moving out of the state. Disloyal bastards."

The AG brightened. "At least the heirs of billionaires seem to be staying. In particular, the grandchildren of billionaires past seem to have developed a keen sense of entitlement, and have disregarded Postrel's warnings." He offered his own version of a joke. "We are about to give them something that's referred to in the field of education as 'a teachable moment.'"

The governor laughed although he did not find it half as humorous as his AG. Still, when a fool has money, you have to hurry to be the one who parts them.

The AG's mood darkened once again. "I came to talk with you about some of the millionaires who were not at the top of our list before, but who have come up as the others departed. They could be a problem."

"Like who?"

"All the big companies and their CEOs who haven't yet committed to moving to Red States. Fact is, we need them."

The governor raised his eyebrow. This was an astonishing confession coming from the AG. "What kinds of companies?"

"GPlex, FB, others like them. I'm thinking about going ahead and running forfeitures on their CEOs anyway. It's not like they could move to a Red state—they're pretty much chained here so they can take ferries and copters out to meet with their teams on the BrainTrust. They really can't get away."

"Please reflect." The governor just sat and stared at his AG until the AG figured out the pesky little problem.

"Oh, right. They could just move everything to the BrainTrust." The AG frowned. "I guess we have to leave them alone."

"Will they believe that we'll leave them alone?"

The AG shrugged. "We'll tell them. We'll give them a written commitment of immunity to forfeiture if necessary."

"It would look really bad if they told the other companies, or worse the media, about their special treatment."

The AG agreed reluctantly. "I suppose." He pondered the matter for a moment, then snapped his fingers. "Got it. We'll send the immunity guarantee in a 'California Security Letter,' with a non-disclosure clause. Anyone who violates the non-disclosure clause gets hard jail time."

The governor nodded appreciatively. "Just like the National Security Letters the feds have been sending out for decades. Deals forced upon the corporations to violate their customers, that are required by law to be kept secret. Excellent." He had another thought. "What about the venture capitalists? So many big companies need them to get started, shouldn't we give them a pass too?"

The AG swung back into normalcy with a fierce glare. "We can't be offering giveaways like this to everybody. We have to draw the line someplace." He choked on his next words. "Maybe a couple of them. If they promise to fund some startups created by unemployed people. But not a lot of them."

"Sounds like a reasonable compromise."

"I'll send you a draft list of California Security Letter recipients this afternoon." The AG had risen from his chair when he remembered something. "Oh, one last thing. It turns out there is at least a little good news about all the departing billionaires."

The governor gave him a look of astonishment. "Good news? Who are you, really, and what have you done with my Attorney General?"

The AG chuckled. "Okay, okay. Take a look at this." He slaved the wallscreen to his tablet and popped a graph. "This is the inequality chart over time. You know we keep this in real-time now. It's too important not to keep up to date."

The governor nodded. He looked at it himself several times a day.

"Okay, so here's the way things used to work before Postrel's article. As you can see, every time there was a big recession, the equality would soar as the stock market collapsed and the wealthy became less so. Then when the Fed started printing money, it would pop the stock market faster than the rest of the economy, so the *inequality* would soar to new highs." He pointed further along the line. "Then the rest of the economy would start to catch up as the stock market plateaued and unemployment fell, and the equality numbers would improve once again."

The governor nodded impatiently. "Yes, yes, as

predictable as a game of billiards. Old news. What's different now?"

The AG pointed yet again. "Here's where Postrel published her article on forfeiture. As you can see, ever since inequality has been falling. Getting rid of the billionaires, even if they escape forfeiture, is really improving our equality numbers."

The governor had started to smile, and the smile had expanded into a grin. "With equality improvements like these, I'm looking at a ten point rise in the polls. This is magnificent."

The sound of the introducer announcing him interrupted the governor's reverie. He went to the podium, waving for his adoring fans. "As you know, we are here to announce the start of the Affordable Child, Worker, and Consumer Protection Program. It will transform our society just as our earlier programs have. But first I want to make an announcement."

He took a deep breath. "On this day, we embark on a bold new journey. Because of new policies and commitments implemented by my administration, we have set a new record for equality in our state. We are going to set more records. At last, we will be able to raise our voices as one. Equality for all!" he shouted.

And the crowd shouted back.

The first few days of any trek, Jam reminded herself, were the hardest. Now she only had a couple of hundred more days to go. The wind whistled across the frost-covered Siberian landscape like cold, harsh laughter.

Jam saw smoke over the next rise and wondered what she would find when she got there. Hopefully, she would find water. Yes, she'd been walking over snow for days, but people who lived with snow knew it was unsatisfactory as a source of water: it took a huge amount of snow to make a little bit of water, and warming it up enough to melt using the heat in her mouth was no fun either. Eating snow slowed the rate of dehydration, but make no mistake, you could die of thirst surrounded by the stuff.

No one had seen her since leaving the dacha, of that she was reasonably sure. A couple of times copters had gone by —big, black, cumbersome things loaded with weapons— but she had been surrounded by trees. They might have found her on infrared, but she suspected such niceties of combat were unavailable to the troops stationed in this part of the backcountry.

The days had not passed unproductively. Jam had learned a smattering of Russian while in the Pakistani Army, enough to curse fluently and demand a beaten enemy surrender, though her fellow troops tended to laugh about needing more to know how, when beaten, to offer a surrender. She had been able to follow the conversation with Tatiana only because of her cell phone and its translator. But for the last three days she had practiced, practiced, and practiced a handful of critical phrases until she thought she might be fluent enough for a short conversation that would not give her foreign origins away. She learned new languages with considerable ease, which was how she'd wound up getting an immersive training in English in the first place. She figured she had at least one chance in twenty of entering the village, buying supplies, and escaping again without too much suspicion.

While practicing Russian, she had also contemplated the big question with no good answer: to buy supplies or steal them? Because her confidence in her Russian had improved, she had decided to buy. She enjoyed having the choice: when escaping from her husband in Pakistan she had not had enough money to make an analytical decision. This time, she had money, having exchanged a wad of Chinese renminbi for rubles before starting her two-woman assault on the Russian empire. If she bought off the locals with large tips, would they stay bought? Vasily could probably tell her. She could call Julissa, have her put Vasily on the phone, and ask him. She should call anyway just to make sure Vasily hadn't murdered everybody and stolen the copter.

Of course, calling anybody was out of the question. If she used her cell, the authorities could track her message traffic even if they could not eavesdrop on her conversation, her phone being of BrainTrust vintage. A phone connection to a BrainTrust location, or anyplace outside Siberia for that matter, would be a dead giveaway. Too dangerous.

It took longer than expected to reach the village: a deep ravine, quite invisible until you were upon it, lay between her and her goal. Going around was easy but time consuming. She entered the store as the sun fell.

Her engagement to procure supplies went surprisingly well. The store owner showed a magnificent lack of interest in anything except her rubles.

The success at the store made her wonder if she were being too cautious. As she passed the little place that seemed to serve as a restaurant, the aroma of real food overpowered her good sense. Hesitating only a moment, she rushed inside and sat down at a tiny table.

A woman approached her. "And so, comrade, what would you like today? I recommend the cooked cabbage with sour cream, and the black bread slathered in butter." The woman scrutinized what little she could see of Jam beneath the coat and scarf. "You need them. Eat up. Calories disappear in the cold."

Jam spoke ever so carefully. "What else do you have?"

The woman smiled so warmly it was hard not to respond. "We also have cabbage with sour cream, and black bread slathered in butter."

Jam smiled back. "I think I'll have that, then."

The woman nodded. "Good choice."

People came and went. Some sat and laughed quietly together. Everyone glanced her way at least once, but left her alone and did not seem ready to confront this odd stranger in town. Jam soaked in the warmth, despite understanding that the more comfortable she became, the harder it would be to leave.

Dinner was delicious. If she'd been served the same food on the BrainTrust, she suspected she would have gagged, but under these circumstances, it was a remarkable repast.

She had just about warmed up when the sound of

trucks rolling to a stop shook the flimsy walls. Conversations throughout the room died. The faces around the tables turned blank or, in the case of some of the younger patrons, downright sullen.

Two men in uniforms barged through the door. Jam put her hand to her ear to make sure the earbud connecting to her cell phone translator remained in place and well concealed.

"We are looking for a criminal who killed a guard and made off with two prisoners," the taller one bellowed. He stared around the room. "Have any of you seen any strangers, yesterday or today?"

One of the sullen men muttered back, in a voice meant to be heard. "Funny, that's not how I heard it. I heard some woman prisoner got into a fight with the guard trying to molest her, killed him, and took off with her daughter. The guard must have been a pansy."

A low murmur of uncomfortable laughter spread around the room.

The shorter man spoke. "As usual, most of the truth has been lost in the retelling." He glanced up at his boss and grimaced. "Though there is reason to suspect the assailant was a woman, not a man."

The boss raised his hand as if to smack his subordinate but restrained himself. "The great detective here thinks he is the Sherlock Holmes of Siberia. I knew Alexei well. No woman could take him. Certainly not like that."

The shorter man did not relent. "The tracks leading in this direction looked like a smaller person's footprints. And we picked a swatch of cloth from a tree that might have belonged to a scarf." His roving eyes found Jam and focused on her. "A scarf that looks a great deal like *your* scarf." He walked over to her table to inspect her more closely. "And who are you? When did you arrive here?"

Jam closed her eyes for a moment, working up a sense of fear adequate to cause her hands to shake for the soldier. Now she would have to kill both of these men from the gulag, and she'd have to kill any other guards outside. She really didn't want to kill these perfectly fine villagers, but did she have a choice?

Of course she had a choice. Of course she would not kill them. Of course they would have to betray her when more guards showed up.

Well, at least she could make some good miles with one of their trucks and all of the corpses in the back.

The woman who had served her thumped up next to him. "You've been following the wrong footsteps. This is my niece. She, unfortunately, did *not* kill the guard who molested her. Toma here hasn't spoken since. She often wanders in the woods." She waved her hands towards the door. "There is no one here for you. This is not the woman you are looking for. Move along."

The boss growled. "Good advice. Like I said, we're looking for a man." He barked at his subordinate, who reluctantly followed him away.

The quiet in the restaurant remained deafening until they heard the trucks fire up and rumble away. The sullen young man who'd told the rumor of the escape slapped his knee. "That was great, Dinara. 'This is not the woman you are looking for.' Ha! Straight from the classics!" He raised a glass in Dinara's direction. "To your health!"

Jam noticed that she did not have a glass to raise, and

there was little to gain from being quiet anymore; quite the opposite in fact. "Dinara, please bring me a vodka. Please bring everyone a vodka, on me!"

At this, everyone raised a glass to Jam's health.

The once-sullen, now-laughing fellow pointed at her. "Is it true? Did you kill the famous Alexei?" He scowled. "That pig from the Spetsnaz?"

"He was holding a gun to the head of a little girl," Jam answered. "I was lucky."

Someone shouted, "To your luck!" That started another round of toasting.

Jam finished her vodka and laid a large wad of cash on the table. "Thank you, Dinara and everyone, so much for your help. I can never repay you. But I should leave now. They'll be back in the morning."

Dinara put her hands on her hips. "You should stay the night."

Jam shook her head. "Thank you, but I have already brought you enough danger." She hesitated, then asked Dinara for a pen. She wrote a phone number on the napkin. "If you wind up in serious trouble, call this number. Tell them Jam asked that they help you."

Dinara looked at the number, puzzled. "Where does this go?"

"It goes to a person on the BrainTrust." Jam hoped to be alive and in the right place to see Colin's face when he received that phone call.

One more salute followed. "To the BrainTrust!" Apparently, even here in Siberia they knew of Jam's home. It made her heart feel a little warmer, a little fuller.

Jam snuck out as another round of drinks made its way through the room.

She had gone less than a kilometer when a whooshing sound rolled overhead, and a spotlight lit her up like a helpless deer. She held up her hand against the glare. Great. Now she'd have to break out of a gulag. Or, more probably, wait for Ping to break her out. Or wind up in the cemetery in a few hours.

A Russian voice shouted from beyond the glare. "You are a most difficult woman to find when you're trying not to be found, did you know that?" demanded Vasily. "Here, let's get you on board before you freeze to death."

She had just closed the cockpit door against the wind when her phone sang, *"Hey now, you're an All-Star."* Jam whipped out the phone. "Dash, are you crazy? You know they can trace this call."

Dash's voice sounded soothing. "Don't worry Jam. I helped Matt put up a new cell phone satellite network. You're talking directly to a cell tower on a satellite. They don't even know."

Jam breathed a sigh of relief. "Good enough."

"So, where are you, so I can send someone to rescue you?"

Jam paused, confused. "Wait. You didn't send Vasily?"

"Vasily?"

"Yes, he just found me and picked me up. We're heading back to China now."

"Vasily? The same Vasily who…" Dash's voice faded as her consternation mounted.

Well, this was complicated. "I'm afraid so, Dash. That Vasily."

Vasily decided at that moment to complicate things further. "Dr. Dash, nice to hear your voice again. Let me apologize once more for…what happened…in the past."

Silence on the phone greeted this apology.

Jam tried to reassemble the pieces of the conversation. "Vasily was very helpful protecting Gleb's family, it turns out."

Dash digested this for a moment. "Alexei?"

Jam had better news on that, sort of. "He's dead."

Vasily chortled. "You should have seen Jam shoot him down. It was a remarkable display of…uh…"

Jam put her hand over her face, wishing Vasily were less helpful, contemplating shooting him now. No good; he was piloting the copter. "It seems Vasily has had a change of heart. Sort of like, you know—"

Dash finished the sentence. "Dmitri." Dash sighed so loudly Jam could hear it. "So I didn't have to persuade Matt and Ben and Amanda and Colin to spend billions of dollars after all."

Jam didn't fully understand this, but she knew the right answer. "I'm so sorry, Dash."

Dash chuckled. "Well, it is a good investment anyway. At least we will all get rich. Or rich*er*, as the case may be."

Jam stared at her phone. "That's the spirit. Look on the bright side."

After they broke the connection, Vasily voiced his personal worries. "What are you going to do with me now? Send me back to Dmitri?"

Jam looked at him like he belonged in a zoo. "You're kidding, right? You belong to me now."

After a moment, Vasily nodded. "Yes, I guess I do."

Silence engulfed the cockpit. Eventually, however, Vasily asked wonderingly, "She spent a billion dollars to get a phone call through to you?"

Jam shrugged. "It's Dash."

9

CRADLE OF CIVILIZATION

Giving money and power to government is like giving whiskey and car keys to teenage boys.
—P.J. O'Rourke

Jam spent the first few days back in China reveling in being warm again. They meandered across the countryside, hopping by copter hither and yon to meet the successful Accel test-takers, moving by truck in a drunkard's walk that nonetheless had a specific destination as its goal.

Jam was dozing, half-listening to the sound of gravel crunch under their wheels, when Julissa spoke doubtfully about approaching their destination. "I think we're coming up on Baotong. It's hard to tell. There's no welcome sign, and not even a dot on a map unless you want to count the GPlex satellite view that no one near here has ever seen and doesn't recognize so they can't tell us if this and that are the same."

Jam opened her eyes.

A village of shanties lay before them. She peered at them. At first glance they looked run down. But as she continued to study them odd little details caught her eye, suggesting they might be in better shape than apparent.

This was the place Ping had demanded she find—long ago it seemed. She'd done as Ping asked, interrogating people in the other villages as they passed through. Most had never heard of Baotong, but the ones who had invariably gave her a pensive assessment before saying in a low voice, "Yes, you should probably go there" when Jam asked. Very strange.

Up on the only hill within kilometers sat a nice house, a mansion by the standards of the village beneath. Jam muttered, "Somebody's doing all right here."

Her eyes drifted on to the only part of the landscape with movement. She caught her breath. "Julissa, look at all the machines."

A large wheat field consumed much of the view between the village and the mansion. It was full of battered machines whirring, clanking, and jittering to and fro. Every one of them made her think of the remote control tiller Song had cobbled together. A gaggle of villagers stood to the side, apparently controlling the machines.

Could she have come upon a village where they had another person like Song? Where they respected him for his unusual skills? Ping had been right. She definitely wanted to track down the inventor of those machines.

Several of the villagers saw her and pointed. A tiny,

ancient woman detached from the others and shuffled with surprising rapidity on an intercept course to catch her and Julissa on the edge of the village.

Julissa rolled to a stop next to the elder. Jam hopped out and offered a short bow.

The elder gave her a soft smile. "You may call me Nuan. You must be Ms. Jam, who is not here to lift the poor. We've been expecting you." She nodded her head. "Let us go to my home, I can give you tea while we talk."

Jam opened the door. "May we give you a ride?"

Nuan pursed her lips. "It is too hard to get in and out of these trucks. Let us walk."

Jam shut the door and caught up with Nuan, who was already shuffling down the dirt road. Julissa followed at a distance with the pickup.

Jam asked, "How did you hear about me? Why were you expecting us?"

Nuan laughed, a warm, gentle sound. "You kept asking people how to find us. We do not get out of the village often, but enough. More fundamentally, we've been expecting someone from the BrainTrust for several years now."

Jam almost tripped. "You have? Why?"

"Reading about your ships, it was clear they have been a great success and would inevitably expand. But to expand, they would need more people." She pointed to the field. "People who can build new things out of old ones."

They walked on in companionable silence to Nuan's house, which sat near the edge of the village. Julissa parked the truck, and all three of them entered the home.

Julissa gasped as they stepped over the threshold, but

Jam was not surprised to find that the interior was a substantial step up from the dilapidated appearance of the village from the road. Every inch of the house was neat and clean. The furnishings, while old and battered, had been lovingly maintained. The floor was not dirt. Rather, it was covered in irregular yet beautifully mated flagstones, fitted together by a master worker of jigsaw puzzles.

Nuan motioned them to the small table. A teapot warmed over a bricked-in fire pit full of embers. She brought the tea, then reached into a cupboard to bring down three teacups, each a different shape, each obviously old but well cared for.

Julissa picked up her cup and studied it, her mouth open in amazement. "These cups must be a thousand years old."

Nuan poured the tea, chuckling. "Two thousand."

Now Jam stared at her in amazement. "Two-thousand-year-old teacups?" She lifted hers gingerly, expecting it to disintegrate at the slightest increase in pressure.

Nuan sighed. "Let me tell you a story, handed down through generations by our ancestors." She sat holding her cup in both hands and looked off into the distance. "As you may know, once upon a time the lands of China were ruled by numerous small warlords."

Julissa nodded. "The time of the Warring States."

"Just so." Nuan sipped her tea. "The internecine wars led to endless slaughter. All but the warlords and their generals suffered, including our people in Baotong. It was unacceptable."

She sighed. "Our people in this little village have always had unusual insight. We were thinkers, not doers, and we could outthink just about any problem—except for men with swords. So we decided the warring states had to be brought to heel, and a unified, civilized state needed to rise in their place."

Nuan rose suddenly in dismay. "I forgot the cookies!" After fussing for a couple of minutes in her pantry, she returned with a plate of almond cookies. "We scoured the states and identified the most empathic, most honorable of the young royalty—a child, really, thirteen years old when he became king—Ying Zheng of the state of Qin. We performed as his generals for war, his advisors for creating wealth, and his engineers for building his Wall. The result is generally referred to as the Qin Dynasty."

Julissa blinked herself out of her spellbound state. "But it didn't last. The Qin Dynasty fell after Ying Zheng, renamed Qin Shi Huang—the First Emperor—died. What happened?"

Nuan frowned. "We didn't understand until it was too late, but as Britain's Lord Acton observed thousands of years later, 'Power corrupts. Absolute power corrupts absolutely.' Ying became obsessed, ironically enough, with a quest for the elixir for life—a quest on which you of the BrainTrust are finally making a little progress, millennia later."

She shrugged. "Anyway, his obsession destroyed him. And we knew we had made a terrible mistake. Just as we had assisted in the creation of the first Chinese Empire and its emperor, we then assisted in its destruction."

Julissa knew the rest of the history, of course. "But other dynasties rose. And fell."

Jam added shrewdly, "But they all left you alone."

Nuan gave her a beatific smile. "Exactly." She stared at Jam, piercing her soul with her eyes. "The time has come to try again. We are ready to go with you."

Jam blinked. "Go with me?"

Nuan did not quite laugh at her. "Yes. To the Brain-Trust. Or rather, to the Fuxing."

Jam scrunched her face. "I can really only take a few people with exceptional qualifications." She pointed out the window. "Like the person who built all the machines working your wheat field. Could you introduce me to him?"

Nuan did laugh at this. "Ms. Jam, we *all* build machines like that."

Jam goggled, but recovered. "I'll need to test everyone."

Nuan rose. "Of course. As expected." She opened the door.

A dozen villagers stood patiently in a line.

Jam took a deep breath. "Well, this will be interesting." She pulled out her cell phone and opened the Accel testing app.

Julissa laughed gaily. "It certainly will be." She fired up her cell as well.

They started testing as more villagers wandered up. With two phones and each test taking less than fifteen minutes, they tested nine villagers in the first hour.

They all qualified for full scholarships.

After the second hour, Jam called a halt. "Enough! I believe you." She laughed low in her throat. "Everyone's going to the Fuxing."

Now villagers seemed to flow out of every corner of the village, cheering.

As night fell, a middle-aged couple holding hands came up to Jam, who sat alone outside Nuan's residence watching the stars come out. Julissa was inside, talking with Nuan as they spread Jam's and Julissa's sleeping bags on the floor.

The woman spoke. "Good evening, Ms. Jam. It's a beautiful night, isn't it?"

Jam scooted over on the split log upon which she sat to make room for the couple. "It is beautiful, even though it reminds me a little of the place where I grew up."

The couple nodded as if they understood.

Jam took a deep breath. "How may I help you?"

The husband looked sorrowful; the woman, hopeful. She spoke of that hope. "We were wondering if you had ever met or heard of a young Chinese woman about your age, by the name of Liling. We thought she might be on the BrainTrust."

Jam shook her head. "I'm sorry. You have to understand, there are over a hundred thousand people on the BrainTrust."

The couple sat down. The woman took Jam's hand, and the husband spoke. "Shu Shi, I told you it was a longshot."

The wife pursed her lips. "I was just so sure." She drew a deep breath. "When our daughter was just ten years old, she was taken by the provincial governor to be one of his concubines. He was a horrific person, but his sister's husband was in the Politburo." She spoke as if that made it all understandable. "Less than a year later he died from an accidental fall from his second story bedroom window. Shortly after that, we received a bill from the government to pay for the bullet used to execute our daughter. They claimed Liling had committed treason." Now tears glittered in her eyes.

Her husband continued. "We didn't really believe it. Her execution, that is, not the murder. Our daughter was the cleverest little girl in the entire village. It was easy enough to believe she'd killed the governor, but hard to believe she hadn't gotten away. We gathered everyone in the village and calculated that there was a good chance—"

"Seven chances in eleven," the wife interrupted.

"Seven chances in eleven that she had gotten away, and the bullet was just for show."

The mother now continued. "But of course she could not come back here. We did some more analysis and concluded there was a good chance—"

Now the husband interrupted. "Four chances in seventeen."

"Four chances in seventeen, that if she were alive, she would have eventually found her way on to the Brain-Trust." She shrugged. "It's just so hard to believe she's dead. She was so alive; a skinny little thing but so energetic. Everyone always said she bounced around—"

Now the husband and wife finished together, "Like a ping-pong ball." They smiled at each other. "Ping, ping, ping." They hugged, and the wife said, "We miss her so much."

Jam had listened to the story with frustrated sorrow until the story turned to table tennis. Electrified by the grand finale, Jam had trouble not shouting her suspicions. Instead she said softly, "I'll make some inquiries. A skinny little thing, right? Super-fast? You know, she may have changed her name."

The husband nodded. "That would have been wise of her, all things considered."

Jam slipped into Nuan's house, humming with delight.

Nuan and Julissa both stared at her. Nuan said what they were both thinking. "You have a beautiful voice."

Jam looked into the distance, perhaps at something deep within herself. "So they say, when I have something really striking to sing about." She turned back to Nuan, now serious. "Exactly how did you plan we'd move the whole village to the Fuxing? I don't think you have enough trucks and cars to move everyone at once."

Nuan raised her eyebrows. "I was assuming you would figure that out." She sighed. "It could be a little difficult. The mayor will not like it if we all leave."

Jam looked puzzled. "He's not one of you?"

Nuan chuckled. "He's from Beijing. His second cousin's wife has a first cousin on the Politburo."

Julissa asked, "He lives in the house on the hill, right?"

Nuan nodded.

Julissa growled. "Puffed-up bureaucrat."

Nuan nodded.

Jam contemplated the situation. "I have no idea how to move everyone out of the village at once. Perhaps we can talk him into helping us."

Nuan shrugged. Julissa snorted.

Jam straightened her back as if preparing to be

assaulted by a great wave. "I'll go up in the morning. See if I can make an arrangement with him."

Two pairs of skeptical eyes stared at her owlishly.

Jam shook her head from side to side. "And I'll see if anybody on the BrainTrust has an idea." Dash had, after all, sent her the copters, which had proven quite useful once Jam figured out what to do with them.

The mayor of Baotong rolled in his sleep. The peasants were required to rise and work the fields at the break of dawn. The mayor, however, did his best work—creative intellectual pursuits of diverse kinds as befitted his status—while dreaming. His work was too important to be disturbed by the coming of daybreak.

As the sun neared high noon, the mayor lay in bed and contemplated getting up.

A loud knock on his door interrupted his musings.

What could the villagers want from him so early in the day?

He dressed slowly; the peasants could wait. When he finished, he made his stately way down the steps to the entry. He had a snappish comment on his tongue as he opened the door, but he swallowed the attack when he saw the lovely young foreign woman standing there. An even younger Chinese woman, he'd guess an interpreter or some such, stood to her left. The local peasant leader Nuan stood to her right.

The mayor harrumphed. "Yes? What do you want?"

The foreigner bowed politely. "My name is Jam. I've

come in search of particularly bright and enthusiastic people to join the BrainTrust on the Fuxing archipelago."

"Bright and enthusiastic? You'll need to look somewhere besides Baotong. These people are lazy dogs." He pointed out the picture window at the field. "Look at them all, standing around the edges, not one of them out in the field doing a proper day's work. If this field didn't produce the highest yields in the region, I'd send them all to the mines."

He glared at Nuan, hoping to get a reaction, but as usual she gave him no response. The old hag couldn't even understand when she was being insulted. "We're fortunate to have such fertile land, or they'd all starve."

The three women just stared at him for a moment. The mayor grunted in exasperation. The fact was, this Jam person was the most attractive woman he had seen in months. "Well, come in for a cup of tea, and we can talk." He glared at Nuan.

Nuan responded quietly, "Let me prepare the tea for you."

The mayor grunted and led his guests into the dining room to sit down.

Jam started the conversation. "You might have difficulty believing this, but in fact every person in your village has passed our qualifying test. There are some additional tests they will need to pass once they arrive on the Fuxing, but I have confidence that they'll pass with flying colors."

The mayor gaped at her. "Your tests must be broken."

Jam shrugged. "Perhaps. But since they passed, my job is to get them to the Fuxing. There aren't enough vehicles here to transport everyone. I was wondering if you could help."

The mayor couldn't believe his ears. "You want to take my whole village? What would I do for workers?"

Jam paused, then offered softly, "You could come to the Fuxing too. As mayor, I am so confident you would pass the testing we can skip it."

Nuan returned with the tea. "It's a very generous offer."

The mayor accepted his cup. "Ha! I've heard about the cabins on the BrainTrust. All tiny."

Jam persisted. "But you would have one all to yourself. Your villagers will be packed in four to a cabin, at least until they find or create jobs for themselves."

Julissa tapped the elegant white teacup decorated with lotus petals. "You have a beautiful tea service here." She took a sip, looking mischievously over at her boss. "Very modern."

The foreign woman glowered at her underling, then turned a radiant smile on the mayor. "And the cabins are all top of the line, with all the most modern conveniences."

The mayor had to admit that sounded attractive. "How many workers would I have?"

The question stopped the foreigner in her tracks. "We do things a little differently on the BrainTrust. You'd have to, uh, put together a business plan. You might want to learn how things work first. We have this exceptional educational system—"

The mayor had heard enough. "I hardly need to go back to school to learn how to manage workers."

He watched as Nuan looked at Jam with an expression that clearly said, *I told you so.*

He suddenly realized that no one had asked his permission to take his people. They were planning to just leave! He was invited, but they were going to go regardless!

Well, he would put a stop to this right now. "No one is taking my workers anywhere! I'll zero out all their social credit!" He rose in fury. "There's no way out of the country for them!" He straightened in a display of dignity and pointed to the door. "Enough. You have overstayed your welcome."

Nuan apologized profusely, saying that Ms. Jam did not understand what she'd been asking. Thereafter the women departed quietly, though something in the foreigner's eyes left the mayor feeling uncomfortably vulnerable. He marched to his phone and started dialing, and eventually, he got a connection. "This madwoman is going to kidnap all my villagers! Send someone to detain her at once!"

I O

———

ESCAPE ESCAPADES

Tactics without strategy is the noise before defeat.
  —Sun Tzu

Matt barely heard the doorbell, so steeped was he in the numbers before him. He was still amazed at how quickly he'd burned through so much money, but all the ventures were paying off. Dash had been right; his costs were going down, and all the extra revenue was going straight to the bottom line.

The doorbell rang again and he went to the door. "Dash! What an unexpected pleasure." He waved her in. "What can I do for you?"

She followed him into his office. "I need you to pick up on another opportunity." She synced her tablet to his wallscreen, showing him a Titan spaceship with hundreds of passengers boarding, lifting off, landing, and debarking the passengers once more.

Matt watched dreamily. "The intercontinental limo. Forty-five minutes to anywhere on Earth. One of the few goals my predecessor set out that he could never fulfill." His eyes turned hawkish. "The regulatory hurdles with building the spaceports were insurmountable."

Dash smiled mischievously. "Not anymore."

Matt looked into her eyes with a puzzled expression.

"You can put a ship like the *Heinlein* within a hundred kilometers of any coastal city in the world. Think about it, Matt." As Matt shook his head, dazed, she added, "Yet another BrainTrust moment?"

Matt jumped to his feet. "We can do it!" He rubbed his hands together. "Ha! *Ha!*"

Dash laid her tablet on his desk. "And I have just the opportunity for your first passenger service. You can save a whole village from terrible oppression."

Matt eyed her suspiciously. "As usual, you have an ulterior motive."

Dash looked away. "Well, yes, but it is still a good idea." She explained about Jam, the Army unit on her trail, and the village full of people who belonged on the Fuxing; all except the mayor, who planned to force them to stay.

Matt rolled his eyes. "Dash, the Chinese missile defense command will see us coming and blow us out of the sky. It's not like they'd give permission if we asked nicely."

Dash conceded, in her own way. "I think Ted and I might be able to help with that, and the flights won't last very long. You'll launch from the Western Pacific, land in Baotong, then launch again after just a few minutes and make an even shorter trip to the Fuxing."

Matt pursed his lips. "We don't have a capsule capable of carrying a whole village."

Dash pushed another button on her tablet, and a standard SpaceR cargo capsule appeared on the wall. "You almost do, for a short trip like the one from Baotong to the Fuxing. We can modify your regular cargo capsule to load a lot of people. No air recirculation or acceleration couches, but they won't need extra air for a flight this short, and you can keep the g-forces low and still have enough fuel for such a suborbital flight like this."

Matt still looked doubtful.

Dash persevered. "There's really no trouble with financing for this one. Lenora Thornhill will pay for the modifications to the capsule and the Titan that Ted will make. You, of course, will undertake the rescue for free."

Matt snorted. "For free? I will?"

"Of course. It will only cost you a load of fuel if things go well. Keenan is all set to discuss insurance options with you if things go less well. This will be a striking yet inexpensive demonstration of your new passenger service. What do you Americans call it? A publicity stunt?"

That pushed Matt over the edge. One of the criticisms he'd faced lately was that he wasn't flamboyant enough, that he didn't go out on a limb the way his predecessor had done. In one single stroke, he could put that complaint behind him. "So, when do you go to work on the capsule? And what exactly is Ted going to do to my beautiful Titan?"

Diric spoke, though he hated to bother his boss when she was napping. "Ms. Ping, I think we need to stop for gas now. Pretty soon we'll be over the ocean, and there won't be another place to fill up."

Ping popped up in her seat. "What? Uh, sure, right." Her soul snapped back into her body. "You're the expert on where to get gas, Diric. Land wherever."

Diric muttered he as pointed down, "In Somalia. I never expected to see my old country again."

Ping watched as Diric brought the plane into a smooth descent, aiming for a ramshackle little store. As usual, the store had no gas pumps, but as they got closer, she could see the quart and gallon glass bottles used in this part of the jungle to store gasoline. "Good thing these engines can use just about any liquid that burns." She'd have to try vodka for fuel sometime...but not when they were far from home.

Ping had lost track of the hours they'd spent flying across the center of Africa. They'd started about fifteen minutes after Ping got the call from Colin telling her that Jam was in trouble in northern China and Dash was launching a spaceship to get her and the whole village of Baotong out of there. A rescue was afoot, and Ping needed to be in on it.

She had to thank Jam for getting into enough trouble to compel Dash to invent a whole new generation of stealth copters. And she had to thank someone—probably Colin—for teaming her up with someone as insightful as Ciara. Who else, when told that they needed a stealth copter for their mission of peace, would say, "Oh, yeah, we're printing one for you on the *Archimedes* as we speak. After all, we both know that not only do you *want* a fast, stealthy, long-range copter but we also know that you're going to need it. *Why* you'll need it, I can't possibly imagine, but need it you will."

Clearly, Ciara's perception of reality was spot-on.

So here Ping was, teaching Diric to drive a copter using the brutal learn-by-experience method generally abjured by Ciara and her mother. Fortunately, Diric had proven an avid and talented learner.

At first Ping had been afraid they'd run out of gas and have to land in some goddam savage land and fight their way out, but Diric had just laughed. "There's fuel all over the interior of Africa. You just have to know how to look for it." The kid had been right about it all along.

And he was right again. They landed next to the store. A little boy stared at them and their copter in awe. Diric talked with the shopkeepers about buying up almost their whole current inventory of gas.

Ping looked around. Four scruffy young men were eyeing her and her copter without the awe. They looked like hungry wolves who had just spotted dinner.

Ping turned casually in their direction, bouncing lightly on her feet to warm up. She smiled brightly.

Behind her, Diric yelled joyfully, "Abshir! I never thought I'd see you again."

The wolfish young men lost the tension in their muscles. They relaxed, and Ping saw them as merely the adolescent boys they were.

Diric embraced Abshir, explaining, "Ms. Ping, this is my cousin. Abshir, this is my new boss. She pulled me out of the water when my uncle took me to hijack her ships. She's the best thing that ever happened to me."

Abshir thanked Ping for saving his cousin.

Diric clasped his hands pleadingly; he had an idea. "Ms. Ping, can you take Abshir on the Prometheus too? He's really smart, and a good guy."

Ping raised an eyebrow. Somebody who had been about to try to rob a BrainTrust peacekeeper with mad skills struck her as being neither good nor particularly bright. But then, Diric had tried to hijack an isle ship, which on the face of it was a more ridiculous proposition. She smiled at Abshir. "If you make your way to our archipelago off the coast of Nigeria, we can probably find something for you."

Diric clapped. "Abshir, do it. Really."

Abshir looked skeptical but waved to them gaily as they departed.

As Ping brought them back on course, she found herself wondering about Abshir's possible travel arrangements. "So, Diric, if Abshir does decide to come to us, how's he gonna get across Africa? Is there airline service between Somalia and Nigeria? Would he take his car?"

Diric chuckled. "Oh, Abshir doesn't have enough money for a car or an airplane ticket. I imagine he'll walk."

Walk all the way across central Africa? Ping thought about asking if she'd misunderstood but didn't have the heart. She suspected she'd understood perfectly well.

Jam could not sleep. She could not understand how the villagers, all gathered with their tiny bundles in Baotong's version of a town hall, could snore so peacefully. Eventually, she gave up trying to join them and went outside.

In the distance she could see a handful of lights. Squinting, she concluded they could only be one thing: the lights of the encampment of soldiers that people from numerous villages had mentioned. Soldiers who seemed intent on tracking her down.

Jam wondered why no one had simply sent a local policeman to question her if there were a problem. To the best of her knowledge, no one had a complaint with her, except no doubt the headmaster of the web addiction rehab center. Could he possibly have enough clout to send such an immense force after a single woman? What justification could he have used? Perhaps she should find out.

A plan formed in her mind. It was foolish. Ping would certainly approve, which demonstrated its lunacy. But what was the point of having skills if she did not use them from time to time? It would keep her from getting rusty.

Major Zhang awakened to the soft touch of a woman's hand on his cheek. The merest hint of perfume accompanied the hand. At first, he thought he was dreaming.

Then a woman chuckled ever so softly over him. "Wake up, Major Zhang. I think perhaps we should chat."

The major jerked awake and tried to rise, but a gentle hand covered his mouth and held him down with unexpected strength. "No yelling now. I just want to talk."

Zhang relaxed, realizing his best chance of dealing with

this stranger was to get her to relax as well. She removed her hand, enabling him to speak. "My guards?"

"Sleeping. They'll have headaches in the morning, but the experience was educational, for them as well as for me, since one of them answered a few questions before he fell asleep. You should not punish them for this lapse. They'll do you proud in the future, Major, with the wisdom I imparted."

Up to this point the major had seen only the woman's face and hands, apparently floating disembodied. Straining, he could see her outline, clad in a black catsuit. He could also see she was beautiful. He was pretty sure he knew who she had to be. "Ms. Jam?" he croaked.

"Indeed. The woman you've been following so relentlessly. I would very much like to know why."

Since the major would very much like to know why himself, the question gave him pause. He sat up in bed, which caused her to flinch, but she allowed it.

Seeing no reason not to tell her, he began to talk about the headmaster of the addiction camp and his first cousin, the governor of Zhang's province. Jam slipped a backpack to the ground and removed two old teacups and a new thermos. As he spoke, she served tea.

Zhang paused to study the teacup. "This must be a thousand years old."

Jam chuckled again. "Two thousand."

A cup from the Qin dynasty! How did she wind up with it?

"I'll leave them here. You should keep them. There will be no one to use them come morning."

He set the priceless relic down gingerly. "What happens in the morning?"

In the darkness her teeth shone brightly in a wide smile. "Fireworks."

They talked till they had emptied the teacups, with her telling him a bit about her mission in exchange for his candor about his. Hers was a very noble adventure in a very profitable sort of way if they could really educate these peasants with such efficiency. He felt compelled to offer a warning. "We have a proverb, you know. 'It takes ten years to grow a tree, but a hundred years to educate a peasant.'"

She laughed so loud she had to cover her mouth. "I'd like to see you explain that to Lenora," she commented, leaving him to wonder just who Lenora might be.

Jam shifted. "I should go. Must I knock you out, tie you up, and gag you?"

The major considered this. Her undetected presence in his tent suggested she had not asked the question idly. Well, he could reacquire her tomorrow. "You have my word I shall not speak of this until morning."

"Ten minutes is all I'll need." She rose, then paused at the tent flap. "Do come to Baotong tomorrow, Major. About nine o'clock. It'll be a sight you'll want to see so you can tell your grandchildren." Her face turned serious. "Don't be early. I wouldn't want to see you or your men hurt accidentally." She disappeared into the night.

He gave her the ten minutes she requested and more, but her insistence that he arrive punctually at nine was too much. He didn't see how it could hurt to arrive an hour or so early.

11

FLIGHT OF THE BLACK TITAN

Pursue one great decisive aim with force and determination.
　—Carl von Clausewitz

Rain lashed the windows of the High Flight deck of the *Argus*. Werner looked across the frothing water at the Heinlein. What had started as a squall had evolved; gale winds whipped everything in sight. They would be lucky if they didn't end up launching in a veritable tropical depression. Anyone with any sense would postpone the launch.

But sense seemed to be in short supply among his companions. Ted stood next to him, muttering excitedly. "What an excellent test. Looks like the graphene surface is holding up just fine. That doesn't prove it will survive re-entry, but I'm optimistic."

Werner had to confess, he did not quite like the new rocket as much as the old. The regular Titans, made of titanium with their surfaces stressed to glitter like titanium jewelry, were breathtaking beauties. This one was stark black, a color dictated by Ted's stealth coating, applied in all haste in the last forty-eight hours.

Dash was along for the vigil as well, by vidcam from the main BrainTrust archipelago. On the wallscreen adjacent to the window, she nodded. "This storm is just what we need to keep a low profile for the launch. Hopefully, the weather will mask the heat and light signatures of blast-off."

Lightning flashed across the sky. An immense wave surged up, but not high enough to affect the isle ships. Werner looked at Dash with immense satisfaction. "I told you the *Heinlein* would need better stabilizers than normal isle ships, but you didn't believe me. Remember?"

Dash gave him a wide grin of acknowledgment. "I stand corrected. Fortunately, I accepted your ridiculous complaint and loaded the ship with gyroscopic stabilizers."

A copter broke through the low-hanging clouds and zoomed toward the *Heinlein*. Werner yelped. "Who the hell is in that copter? What sort of insane person flies through a storm like this to land next to a rocket that's about to launch?"

On the wallscreen, Dash nearly jumped out of her skin when her phone started playing *No Diggity*—the Anna Kendrick version from Werner's childhood. Dash put the phone to her ear in amazement. "Ping!" Dash listened for a moment. "You're where? You want to do what? Ping, you're flying into a typhoon!"

Werner no longer wondered who was crazy enough to fly a copter here. Given all the stories he'd heard, he should have guessed.

Dash sighed in exasperation. "Werner, Ping needs to get into the space capsule. She's going to help Jam if there's any interference with the departure of the villagers."

Werner stared at her in amazement.

Ted nudged him. "She can get on, right? What's the problem?"

Werner thought about it and blew out a breath. "Let me call the operations officer. If she can land on the *Heinlein* in a typhoon, she can ride on the Titan when it launches in a typhoon."

Dash gave him another warm smile. "Thank you so much, Werner. We all really appreciate this." She disconnected her image from the wallscreen as she got back on the phone.

Soon thereafter Dash hung up and started pacing. Toni, whom Dash had invited to join her for the launch, watched her. "What's wrong?"

Dash wrung her hands. "I need to get to the Fuxing. I just know that somehow they're going to get hurt. I need to be there." She continued pacing.

Toni watched for a few seconds. "This is really important to you? You're really sure you need to go?"

Dash threw up her hands. "Yes, yes, but how? It's just not possible. Even if our copters flew fast enough, they don't have the range." She stopped pacing for a moment. "We need better copters with better power." She slumped. "The new nuclear battery I designed for Colin is too heavy.

We need something better." She turned rueful. "In the meantime, there's no way to get there."

Toni smiled broadly. "Nothing's impossible for the woman with the right friends." She pulled out her cell phone. "Daddy? I need my fighter. To get to the Fuxing. Yes, Daddy, now. Oh, really? You have it parked at Eglin, waiting for me just in case? You're so good to me, Daddy."

Toni pocketed her phone. "My plane should be here in a jiff. I'll take you to the Fuxing. My dad will have to persuade the Americans to give us some midair refueling, but it shouldn't be a problem."

Dash stared at her. "You own a fighter?"

Toni laughed. "Yeah, sort of. A modified F-35, the Adir, custom built for Israel with a second cockpit for a weapons officer. You up for a high-speed, high-altitude plane ride?"

Dash's eyes widened in amazement. Eventually she regained the power of speech. Dash remembered a question she had been meaning to ask, one she had started to ask long ago at Ben's First Launch party. "Who *is* your father, anyway?"

Toni laughed again. "Oh, right. I never told you, did I? He's the Prime Minister of Israel."

Dash took some time to digest this, then moved on to more immediate concerns. "But we don't have an airstrip."

Toni waved the objection away. "It's a VTOL. Think of it as the hottest copter in history. We'll land it on the helipad." She frowned. "We may have to repair the helipad when we're done, but it should work."

Dash's brain went back into high gear. "If this works, I will get Amanda and Colin to resurface all the helipads with graphene-reinforced carbon. Then we will be good to go."

Toni touched her fist to Dash's shoulder. "That's the spirit."

———

Major Zhang tapped the dashboard of the lead truck impatiently. He didn't know what would happen at nine, but he was quite sure he wanted to be there ahead of time. He needed to take this Jam person into custody. The charges? Operating an unlicensed helicopter.

It was a silly charge out here in the middle of nowhere, but hopefully it would be enough to satisfy his superiors.

In fact, he was not at all interested in pressing charges. He just wanted to see her again. He would decide what to do about the charges after seeing her, this time in more favorable circumstances. Which was to say, circumstances under which he had control.

The driver interrupted his ruminations, pointing high into the sky. "Major! Look!"

An enormous fireball came hurtling across the sky. The sight was soon joined by an enormous clap of thunder as whatever-it-was descended.

Zhang remembered her words. "Fireworks," he muttered under his breath. Louder, he added, "Step it up! We must get there before it lands!"

Even as he said it, however, he knew they would be too late.

The forces of the universe conspired once again to deprive the mayor of Baotong of his proper repose.

This morning, daybreak seemed to be occurring with unnatural brightness and speed, accompanied by a loud rumble. The brilliant light and the noise jarred him half-awake, and he stumbled to his feet, eyes still closed, and found the window curtains by feel alone. He pulled the curtains closed, which shut out enough of the light for him to stumble back to bed and go back to sleep.

Jam looked up at the hatch on the capsule, far above her, still coupled to the boosters that had brought it here. The soon to be ex-residents of Baotong were swiftly laying a pattern of flagstones across the charred and barren field that had been wheat mere minutes ago. The ground no longer glowed cherry red, but it was still far too hot to cross without something to protect their feet.

The hatch opened, and a long set of steps unfolded accordion-like from the opening. The metal steps cut in half the distance they would have to cover with stone to board, bypassing the half that was also the hottest. Jam felt considerable relief.

A figure appeared in the hatchway wearing a pack and carrying a collection of folded tubes. Jam goggled at the sight. "Ping! What are you doing here!" she yelled at the top of her lungs.

Ping hopped down the steps two at a time. "Jam!" she shouted back. "We need to hurry!" She shifted her bundle and pointed into the distance. "The army's on its way!"

Jam looked where Ping pointed. Clouds of dust billowed behind Major Zhang's trucks as he rushed to get here before she departed. Well, she'd warned him, and given him a recommended ETA that was late enough so that, if he decided to show early, he'd still be safe.

A little old man laid the last stone, and the villagers started to hurry aboard. Ping somehow skipped over the stones past the passengers without either stepping onto the broiling hot ground nor pushing anyone else. She dropped the tubes—her Big Gun, folded up, of course—and threw her arms around Jam. "You are looking exceptional." She stepped back to scrutinize her friend. "And that dress really makes a statement, girl."

Jam laughed as she twirled, once more displaying the Karl Lagerfeld gown Dash had given her so far away and so long ago. "I still should not have brought it with me on this crazy trip through China—a sensible person would have brought more underwear—but somehow it felt right to wear it today."

Ping gave her a sideways grin. "Well, it certainly does lend the occasion a celebratory air."

The last of the villagers had climbed the last of the steps. Ping picked up her Big Gun.

Jam looked at it in displeasure. "I see you've got your BT12 PGM auto launcher with you. Really, Ping, you need to have Dash surgically attach it to you." She fingered the black pack strapped over Ping's shoulders. "What've you got in the backpack?"

Ping twirled once to show off the pack. "That's no backpack. It's my *batpack*!"

Jam gave her a puzzled look. "Batpack?"

"Yeah, like Batman's utility belt. Everything you could possibly need for the unforeseen. Duct tape, WD-40, stuff like that. I've never flown on an experimental rocket ship rescuing a whole village before, so I brought my batpack." Ping gestured to the ship. "Come on."

She hopped across the stones and up the ladder. Jam moved with more careful grace till she was near the top, then turned to look one last time at the soldiers rushing toward them.

Major Zhang, jouncing up and down as the truck banged along the decrepit road far too fast, tried to watch with his binoculars as Jam climbed the steps. Of course, the binoculars bounced with the truck, nearly poking out an eye. He gave up. He considered giving up the pursuit. Then it dawned on him, what it would mean when Jam finished boarding, and the ladder retracted, and the engines rumbled to life.

More fireworks. Really big fireworks. On the ground. "Halt the convoy!" he yelled into his radio. "Stop now!"

The convoy ground to a halt, not quite skidding as they jumbled halfway off the road. He turned to his driver. "We'll watch from here. This should be a sight for you to tell your grandchildren about." He raised his binoculars to his eyes. This time he was able to hold them steady easily.

She was wearing a ballroom gown, pink, blue, and a dark beige of some sort that no doubt had a very fancy name. The dress fit perfectly, undoubtedly custom-tailored by the best the BrainTrust could offer and certainly worth more than his house. Somehow it was only proper.

At the top of the steps she turned and looked toward his convoy. She could not possibly see him from so far away with no binoculars, but he knew she was looking directly at him.

She waved.

Then she was gone, the ladder was up, and a rumble followed shortly after a belch of smoke and fire lit beneath the ship.

Major Zhang threw open the door and yelled, "Take cover! Take cover!"

Those who heard him threw themselves instinctively to the ground, responding to orders without thought or hesitation. The major himself just stood and watched as the spaceship lifted off and turned once more into a fireball in the sky.

At that moment, Zhang had a ridiculous thought. He realized he was in love.

***

The mayor of Baotong made a raspy sound, his best approximation of a growl. Would no one let him sleep? He opened his eyes in irritation. The thunder had come back even louder this time he thought, and the light was so bright the glare penetrated his curtains. He needed new blinds, he decided.

Rising with a grunt, he went to the window to see what he could see.

The first thing to catch his eye was a bright flare in the

sky. As it faded into the distance the thunder subsided as well, leading him to swiftly deduce that they came from the same source. Odd, but hardly important. He looked down to watch the peasants work in the field, a sight that always cheered him up.

Finally, he realized something was terribly wrong. No peasants worked the growing crops. No crops grew. Where just last night the wheat had risen in waving rows, only charred barren dirt remained.

He did not have much time to stare at the mysterious disaster; a convoy of army trucks sped towards his home. He dressed in haste, worrying about how the army would react when they asked him what had happened—and he had no idea.

Major Zhang directed the convoy up to the comfortable-looking house on the hill, the only comfortable looking place in ten kilometers. Surely this was the mayor's place. He grimaced as he realized that the mayor had been correct, more or less, in his accusations against the foreign woman.

When Zhang jumped from the truck and headed towards the house, a man in office attire, obviously having dressed in haste, charged out the front door. Zhang surmised that the mayor had decided in a very military fashion that his best defense might be a strong offense. "Major! Hurry! That woman I told you about? She's kidnapped all my workers!" He pointed at the charred, barren field. "And she vandalized my wheat!"

Major Zhang listened to this with growing amazement. "You think she vandalized your wheat field? Poured a little gasoline around and dropped a cigarette?"

The mayor spluttered. "I don't know how she did it, but she was certainly responsible." He pointed at the trucks. "Get your men moving! She can't have taken my workers far! Get them back! And arrest her!"

The major turned to look back to where the dust thrown up by his trucks still hovered, floating lazily in the still air. "You want me to go after them with the trucks?" He reluctantly started to laugh. His lieutenant had meanwhile caught up, and the major repeated, choking on his laughter, "He wants me to go after them with the trucks."

The lieutenant stared, then started to laugh as well.

Zhang pulled out a cell phone.

The mayor grunted. "You won't get a signal out here. Those incompetent phone people refuse to put up a tower." This was clearly one of the mayor's pet peeves—being cut off from civilization like that.

The major pulled out a second phone, muttering to himself. "Curious. Jam's phone works." He contemplated it for a moment. Should he make the call with the phone that worked? The BrainTrust phone? No, better not. He put the phone away and addressed the mayor. "You have a landline? I have to call the Air Force."

The mayor shook his head, startled. "The *Air Force*?"

This dunce had been annoying the major for hundreds of kilometers, and for days on end. Now the dunce had lost his whole village, and he was acting like he's the victim! Major Zhang approached him and yelled, "The Air Force, you ninny! We've been invaded! You are clearly a collaborator! Hurry, now, or I'll have you in chains!"

The mayor hurried. The major started making calls.

———

The general in command of China's Ballistic Missile Early Warning System was drinking a Grande Starbucks Americano when one of his trackers, who was watching the returns from the Changcheng infrared sensor satellites, shouted, "Unidentified missile launch!"

The general nearly jumped out of his chair. He managed to stay firmly seated, and asked calmly, "Where?"

The tracker spoke this time with considerably less confidence. "From the Loess Plateau, General."

The general shouted in astonishment, "From *inside* China?"

"Yes, sir." The tracker paused. "The signature approximately matches that of a Kestrel Heavy triple booster."

While the general puzzled over this, another officer monitoring the communications of the other early warning systems networks by the other major powers spoke. "Traffic analysis suggests the Americans are going to Defcon 3."

The hair on the back of the general's neck rose. From the American perspective, it could easily look like the Chinese had just launched an ICBM.

The tracker announced, "I've lost it, sir. The boost phase has ended."

The general rose from his chair. "Radar! Have you got it?"

"Sir! No radar tracks!"

No radar tracks? A stealth missile?

The radar operator spoke again. "Wait, I've got something… It's sporadic." He watched for another moment, then continued, "It's similar to the tracks left by our stealth fighters, General." Another pause. "I think this rocket is shedding its stealth coating."

The general nodded. The Chinese fighters were notorious for losing their stealth due to time and poor maintenance. This rocket was losing its stealth to the more brutal force of launch to orbit.

The radar operator continued, "We have calculated the rocket's splashdown location, which will be in the ocean southeast of Hong Kong." He checked the map. "Probably heading to the new BrainTrust archipelago, the Fuxing."

The comm net monitor spoke. "The Americans are standing down from Defcon Three."

One of the general's telephones rang. He picked it up. "Who's this?" he demanded abruptly. "Zhang? *Major* Zhang? Who the hell are you?"

Major Zhang rubbed his temples. "I'm an Army officer currently in the village of Baotong. Don't bother to look it up. You won't find it on any of your maps unless you can find Nowhere in the Middle of Nowhere."

The mayor whined. "It's my village. Very important."

Quite inattentive to the mayor's needs, Zhang continued speaking on the phone. "You may have just detected a missile launch from here. It looked like a Kestrel

Heavy, or maybe one of those new Kestrel Titans, except it was black." He paused, ruminating. "It might have a stealth coating."

Zhang listened for a moment. "Yes, that sounds about right. Anyway, I watched everyone from the village board the rocket before it departed. I was too far away to stop or question them, but I had a clear view of the event."

The mayor screamed for the benefit of the man on the phone, "Kidnapped! My workers were all kidnapped!"

Zhang closed his eyes. "That's the mayor. He's quite confident his people were kidnapped by a foreign woman." He paused. "The mayor's second cousin's wife has a first cousin on the Politburo."

This was a calculated insult. When political personages explained the family relationships that gave them power, they described them as a means of giving themselves prestige. When a military man explained such a relationship to another military man, it was a quiet way of highlighting the individual's incompetence.

"Yes, General, they invaded our country. And left." He rubbed his temples again as the general spoke. "Perhaps, General. But if the nation is invaded by a bus, and some people take the bus back where it came from, are the passengers guilty of any crime?" More words spilled from the phone. "Very well. Yes, I can take care of things on this end easily enough."

Major Zhang hung up the phone and stared into the distance. "You'll need to find more workers, Mayor. One way or the other, I don't think your villagers are coming back."

The general stood with his lips pursed for a long moment. The rocket was full of Chinese peasants? It made no difference. The rocket had violated Chinese airspace. Peasants were unimportant, but airspace was sacrosanct. "Somebody get me the Air Force base outside Shanghai! Scramble a squadron of fighters! We have to shoot that spaceship down!"

Jam stood next to Ping by the hatch, holding onto a stanchion for dear life. The takeoff had been low gee, quite gentle as Jam understood rocket launches to be, and now Jam's feet were floating off the deck; she was weightless.

Ping was laughing her fool head off. "I just love this stuff!" She looked around at the people squashed into the capsule. "Even if it does feel like the Chicago El at five in the evening. They say the BrainTrust is a sardine can. Ha! Try the El."

Jam looked around. To her, the BrainTrust did indeed seem packed with people, and the crush here in the capsule seemed insane. Waziristan was a land of vast spaces filled with rock. This was a whole new experience, even without the zero-g.

It did not last long. She felt the capsule rotate, a distant rumble reached her, and her feet floated gently to the deck again.

Ping sighed. "Well, fun while it lasted. We'll have to do it again sometime."

Gravity returned to normal. Jam let out a breath she hadn't realized she'd been holding.

Ping chattered on, "Assuming this landing is like the last one, we don't have long to—"

A terrible explosion reverberated through the ship and another sudden acceleration struck them, much stronger but shorter than the one that had lifted them from Baotong.

Ping guessed the cause. "I think the main boosters just blew up, and the emergency booster just beneath us ejected our capsule from the rocket." A short popping sound came from overhead, followed by a jerk, then gravity steadied once more. "That would be the parasail deploying."

Jam still clung to the stanchion. "Are we safe yet?"

"Look on the bright side. Not much left to go wrong," Ping chirped.

Air Force Captain Gao carefully restrained his glee. His squadron would get to shoot down an enemy! An invader! China had had far too much peace in the last decades, so this was an extraordinary opportunity.

And it could be a challenge since the enemy target was stealthed. And half his squadron was down for maintenance, though the description of the target suggested this would be no problem at all. Mostly, he expected this to be fun target practice. And to the best of his knowledge, no one had ever shot down a landing rocket ship before. He'd be first!

His fighters came into the battlespace at a low cruising speed. They needed to find the enemy before kicking it up.

Being unable to get a good radar lock slowed down his squadron only moderately, since the search coordinates were tight. Soon enough one of his fighters called, "Two o'clock high."

Gao looked, and sure enough, a three-booster rocket was plummeting down. Its long thin black body was easy to see against the blue sky. Even better were the brilliant fires of the engines braking her descent. No radar, but the choice of weapon was obvious. "Infrared homing missiles." He flipped the safety guards off his weapons toggles. "I'll just get this, and we can go home."

He fired. The missile scooted off at Mach 3 and struck the exhaust nozzle of a side booster. The entire thing blew up.

A rousing chorus of congratulations filled the radio waves, but as the squadron veered away, a smallish part on the top, the capsule, cleared the fire and debris. It popped a parasail. The chute spun, then held steady as it brought the capsule gently down.

Glancing down, Gao could see the BrainTrust fleet, clearly the capsule's target. "Hold on, men. We're not done yet."

Gao led his squadron in a circle and pondered the situation. Radar was not working adequately: it could see the parasail, but could he get enough damage to make a difference shooting up that enormous surface? Meanwhile, the capsule seemed to have no heat signature—that black skin must have radiated the heat from reentry with incredible efficiency. He could have used vidcam-guided missiles, but none had been included in his loadout. Perhaps he was just rationalizing, but he thought he had a compelling justification to fulfill a fantasy. "Use the rapid-fire cannons, everyone! We'll chew it up."

Jam heard, just dimly, surging engines. "Are there planes nearby?"

A staccato sound accompanied the roar, a sound she recognized. "Cannons!"

A dozen holes appeared in the fuselage of the capsule, and shouts of alarm went up. Jam couldn't tell if anyone was seriously injured.

Ping grunted. "Ow. They're shooting at us." She ran to the hatch, threw open the door, and unhitched her Big Gun.

Jam's eyes widened in alarm. "Ping, you shoot that thing from here, the backblast will kill everyone."

Ping growled as she set the gun, still folded up, on the deck. "I know, I know." She whipped off her batpack, wrenched open a zipper, and started pulling stuff out.

Jam shook her head. "Rope? You brought *rope*?"

"Aside from duct tape and WD-40, what else is more useful in emergencies?" Ping whipped the rope around one ankle, then the other, in an intricate knot. "I just wish the rope were longer. I have to hang down far enough to clear the emergency engines, so I'm going to have to hang upside down and use the length of my body as part of my rope." As she dogged off the knot, she muttered to herself,

"Upside-down, he says. Practice upside-down. He should know. But do I listen?"

Wind noise made hearing difficult. Jam yelled, "*What?*"

"Nothing." Ping threw the other end of the rope to Jam. "Tie this down someplace close to the hatch. Really close."

Jam looked up at the stanchion to which she clung, which was too far away to be ideal. After scanning the area nearer the hatch, she sighed, grabbed the rope, and struggled with her elegant gown to wind the rope around her thighs, between her legs, and around her waist, as they'd taught her in the commandos for making a quick and dirty climbing harness.

At last she was ready. The gown had not been damaged irreparably, she hoped.

Ping grinned. "Hold me. Don't let go."

Jam finished tying off, grabbed both sides of the hatch, and nodded to her friend. Ping slid backward over the side, holding the Big Gun in one hand, paying out rope with the other. She grunted once as her feet went over the side, and she bounced against the side of the capsule several times as she unreeled the rope. Jam heard her shout something which was no doubt pithy, but the words were lost.

The fighters were coming back for another pass. Ping was still assembling her gun as the fighters started their run. Jam groaned. "Too late," she shouted futilely.

Then three of the fighters exploded in midair, and the other three veered off in all directions.

Toni had kept up a running chatter over the onboard intercom with Dash when they first lifted off from the helipad on the *Chiron*. But even at fighter speeds the trip was long, and repeated midair refueling slowed them more. Toni had to grin at the thought of the American tankers helping them. If they knew that the fighter they were refueling carried the woman the Chief Advisor desperately wanted to kidnap, they'd have apoplexy.

But finally they came into visual range of the Brain-Trust Fuxing. "Dash, we're almost there."

"I know I need to stop thanking you for this, but I cannot help thanking you one more time. Thank you."

Toni laughed. "Like I said, I've been looking for an excuse to take her for a spin." Warning lights started going off; she looked more closely at her instruments. "We have company. Half a dozen Chinese fighter planes—ha! Chengdu J-20 stealth fighters, the most visible stealth fighters ever built—are vectoring in..." She studied her sensors in surprise. She couldn't see the Chinese fighters' target on radar, but...she looked where her infrared was tracking an enormous signature. "Those shmucks! They're gonna to shoot down the spaceship!"

Dash shouted. "What? Can they do that?"

Toni heard new warning tones and watched on her zoom viewer as a missile plowed into the firing engines. The whole rocket disappeared in a ball of flame. "Dammit!" Then she saw the parasail pop open; soon the capsule swayed gently beneath it. Toni spoke with relief. "It's ok, Dash, they survived."

Next she saw that the fighters were circling around for another pass. She glanced down at her instruments. She whooped. "My dad is the greatest! He gave me a full weapons load!" She flipped on the afterburners as she yelled at Dash, "Don't worry! We're going to save them!"

The afterburners drove them into their seats as they accelerated, pushing past Mach 1 and climbing to 1.6. As they drove full-bore into the battlespace, Toni fired all four of her AMRAAM missiles at different targets. Three of the enemy fighters disappeared in small fireballs of their own. "Missed one," she announced more cheerfully than probably made sense. "And now we're in a knife fight. This is going to be interesting." She shouted to Dash, "Hang on! Try to scream as little as possible!"

Gao was happily leading his fighters into the next firing pass when three of his planes disappeared from the radar display. Someone yelled, "We're under attack!" Gao stared at his screens and ordered, "Stealth fighters! Scatter! Find targets!"

Dash grabbed the chest straps of her harness and held on. From a physics perspective, she realized this made her no safer, but it felt more secure.

As the plane started to jink—like Ted's copter, only more viciously—she heard herself screaming. She wasn't sure whether she was screaming in excitement or terror.

Over the intercom, she heard Toni screaming too, but it sounded more like laughter.

Gao heard one of his men shout, "I see one. Got a radar return." Silence for a moment, then, "It's an F-35." The voice turned puzzled. "Or not. Odd bird." Now the voice turned to alarm. "Nails! It's on your tail!"

Gao finally got a flickering radar return off the bandit. It seemed like an F-35. Good stealth on the approach, but once in a dogfight you could get radar hits off the sides.

He banked to come to his wingman's aid but saw he was going to be too late.

Toni ceased fire with her GAU-12 Gatling gun and whooped. "Score four!" She studied her screen. It took little analysis to reach a grim conclusion. Her fighter, with its modifications to accommodate a Weapons System Officer in the second cockpit, was less maneuverable than a standard fighter. Without missiles or stealth or surprise left, the remaining two enemy craft were swinging slowly but surely behind her. "Dash, there's a red and yellow striped handle by your right hand. When I yell for you to pull it, you pull it with all your strength. *All your strength!* You got me?"

Toni barely heard Dash's acknowledgment as she banked under the capsule. If she could get the two fighters to spend their remaining munitions on her, perhaps the spaceship would survive. She dipped down, then started to climb. She saw an enemy fighter settle on her tail and braced for the inevitable.

Then the fighter behind her disintegrated. Moments later its companion disappeared in a fireball, blocking her view of the capsule.

Ping swung like a pendulum from the rope that was anchored to the capsule, which itself swung like a pendulum from its parasail. Occasionally the rhythms of the two pendulums interfered, causing Ping to twist in a sudden sharp bounce beneath the ship.

She cursed with speed and fluency. The Big Gun proved harder to unfold into firing position when you were unfolding it upside down, and she realized that she was fighting the gravity. "Dummy," she muttered, "*Use* the gravity, don't fight it."

She flipped the gun over so that it was right-side up with respect to the Earth, although it was now upside-down to her. Shaking it vigorously, the tubes smacked her in the face only three times before the final piece locked into place. "Argh. Need to make a note about that in the Big Gun evaluation." She spun around seeking targets. "Where are they now?" She held the digital scope to her eyes. "Come on, come on, bring me some."

She heard the roar of jet engines behind her; a fighter sizzled beneath and started to climb right before her eyes. She zeroed in, then stopped. "Huh? An F-35? No…What the hell?"

Another plane tore past her, chasing the first. This one was clearly Chinese. "Gotcha," she muttered as she pulled the trigger twice, launching a pair of missiles up the sucker's tail exhaust.

Another plane followed. Ping was in her groove; she popped off two more missiles faster than before. "Ooops. Too close. Shit," she muttered as the plane exploded in her face.

Jam stood braced in the hatch, marveling as she watched Ping blast a fighter out of the sky. Ping was going to be absolutely insufferable after this.

Or not. The last fighter banked as it passed beneath their capsule, and when Ping's missile struck it was too close. The shockwave threw Jam from the spaceship.

Jam then realized that there was something far more stupid than jumping from a perfectly fine airplane with a parachute. It was falling from a perfectly fine spacecraft without a parachute. Down she went, screaming curses in Pashtun at the top of her lungs.

She was still screaming when she became aware that Ping was reeling her in with the rope as fast as she could. Jam then heard Ping's voice over the rushing wind. "Get down here!" Jam thought she was going down fast enough already, thank-you-very-much, but she did as Ping requested, pulling on the rope with the same frenetic zeal as her partner. They reached each other in moments. Ping shouted, "Hang on!" Only then did Jam notice a ripcord now sticking out of an unsealed compartment in Ping's batpack. As Ping pulled the cord, Jam clung to her frantically.

Jam was rewarded with a satisfying jerk to her shoulders as the airfoil snapped open. She tried to take control of her limbs, shivering with excess adrenaline.

Ping grunted. "Crap. Too much weight and I can't get control. Hang on."

Jam had no problem obeying. She held on for dear life. "A parachute? You carry a parachute as part of your general-purpose emergency kit?"

Ping grunted again, still focused on trying to get control of their descent, albeit with minimal success. "Not usually, but going up in the air on an experimental spacecraft? You betcha. Besides, Batman does it all the time."

They spun down to the sea, going too fast, never quite gaining control, and crashing into the water with stunning impact.

Coming out of a daze, Jam surmised that she was still alive, but concluded it wouldn't last long because she couldn't breathe. She looked around, oriented on the bubbles that were presumably headed up, and kicked to the surface.

Where was Ping? She lay face down in the water. Jam crossed the waves as fast as she could and flipped her friend over.

Ping coughed. "Thanks." She looked around. The ships of the Fuxing were out of sight.

Jam pointed over Ping's shoulder, "Looks like that may be our best shot over there."

Ping rotated, then gurgled when a wave hit her while she laughed in delight. "Oh goody. It's a Chinese cruiser."

Jam spoke sourly. "Well, it's better than drowning, I suppose, but I was hoping not to be taken prisoner when I got up this morning."

Ping looked at her in puzzlement. "Prisoner? What are you talking about?" She pointed at the cruiser, now clearly bearing down on them. "We just capture it and take it back to the BrainTrust."

Capture it. Of course, that would be Ping's plan. Why hadn't Jam thought of that?

Jam opened her mouth to start listing the reasons why capturing the cruiser might not be as easy as it sounded, but the list was so long she couldn't decide where to start. And she could already hear Ping's counterpoint to each objection. In the end, there was only one thing to say. "Ok."

They started swimming toward the cruiser. When Jam realized that Ping was having trouble keeping up, she paused and looked back at her companion. "What's wrong?"

Ping grimaced. "Nothing. Just grazed by a piece of shrapnel when those bullets hit the capsule."

Jam now saw a slight reddish tint to the water.

Ping pointed at the cruiser. "You go on. I'll catch up. Don't capture the cruiser until I join you."

Jam shook her head. "Let me help you."

Jam had just reached Ping when they both saw the shark fin at the same time. "Damn," they said in unison. A second shark fin joined the first.

Ping spoke again. "Ok, like I said. You go on. It's me

they want. After I take them out, I'll be with you in no time."

Jam spun till her back was against Ping's, giving them a full 360 degrees of coverage. "We'll take them out together," she replied grimly.

"Whatever."

Jam had one shark in her sights when she felt Ping jerk. Ping shouted, "Score! Kick 'em in the nose. They don't like that."

Jam kicked and missed, but so did the shark. It ripped a big piece out of Jam's gown and turned away. Jam screamed. "My dress! The shark took a bite out of my dress!" The shark circled back for another pass; this time Jam hammered it in the nose. "My dress is ruined!"

Ping shifted against her, kicking again. She turned philosophical. "Well, Jam, if you're going to wear a beautiful gown to go skydiving and swimming, you have to expect things like this to happen."

Jam watched as two more shark fins appeared. "Uh, Ping?"

"I see 'em." Ping continued after a pause, "We'll have to take care of them faster, or they'll outnumber us."

"We may need a better plan. I confess—"

A sound similar to the clap of a detonation rose through the water, lifting them both up before dumping them back down. The shark fins disappeared.

Jam felt herself being lifted on a rubbery surface; it made her think of the skin of the dolphin she had once touched near the BrainTrust, which had felt sort of like a hard-boiled egg. As the surface rose it curved; Jam slid stickily down the side. Pretty soon she was able to see enough of the object to make it out: a very large torpedo or a small submarine, big enough to hold several people.

A hatch opened, and Security Chief Baddeley stuck his head out. "You two need a lift?"

Once they'd gotten Ping stretched out on a bunk inside the mini-submarine, she started asking questions. "Did the spaceship make it? Is everyone ok?"

Hart assured them that, although the capsule had missed the helipad on the *Taixue* for which it had been aiming, it had hit the water in one piece just off the stern. The catamarans had unloaded everyone before the capsule started sinking.

Ping went on to the next subject. Rather than passing out from loss of blood, she seemed to have become feverish. "What about the Chinese cruiser? Are they going to give us any trouble?

Hart glanced at his instruments. "They seem to have lost interest in us after we dived. We're at two hundred meters so we may have a thermocline hiding us. Or they have more important fish to fry." His voice turned grim. "They seem to be heading straight for the archipelago."

Ping closed her eyes at last and Jam took over Hart's interrogation, waving her hands in all directions. "Where did this come from? I didn't know we had submarines."

Hart shook his head in bemusement. "Yeah, we didn't until a few days ago. This just got here from the BrainTrust proper. I guess it was a pet project of Colin's." He paused. "I get the feeling Dash helped too. I'm told she designed the power supply."

With her eyes still closed, Ping smiled. "Of course."

Hart continued to speak to Ping. "They tell me there's another sub on its way to the Prometheus fleet, so you'll have one when you get back on station."

Ping's smile widened as visions of submarine warfare danced in her head.

Jam had one more question. "And finally, who was the lunatic who took on a squadron of Chinese fighter planes by himself?"

Hart laughed out loud. "Now *that* is a funny story. Toni Shatzki was flying Dash out here in case anybody needed patching up after the rescue. Anyway, Toni ran into the Chinese shooting at you. She said she had no choice but to fight her way through."

Jam and Ping almost screamed in unison. Jam: "Toni went into that dogfight with Dash on board?" Ping: "Dash is here on the Fuxing?"

Hart raised his hands defensively. "Whoa, folks! I don't make the news, I just report it." He looked at Ping, who had closed her eyes again. "All in all, I think it's a good thing Toni brought Dash out, for more than one reason."

Jam looked down at her now-unconscious friend and had to concur. Then she realized they still had a problem… The Chinese cruiser was about to attack the very ships where Dash awaited them.

INVASION

The supreme art of war is to subdue the enemy without fighting.
    —Sun Tzu

Captain Han Chunlan, commander of the Chinese cruiser *Renhai*, accepted his orders with cautious excitement. He'd been shadowing this clutter of BrainTrust isle ships for months, forced to stand back and allow them to violate Chinese waters with not the slightest concern in their little BrainTrust heads. Certainly, he should have been allowed to fire a few warning shots when they first anchored here, making them scamper somewhere else for safety. *Anywhere* else.

But the Politburo had been leery of starting a war with the BrainTrust, and Captain Chunlan could understand their reasoning. With their ships sitting at the very nexus of conflicting claims between China, the Philippines, and the rebels of Taiwan, a shooting war with the BrainTrust could easily explode into a regional war of epic proportions.

But that didn't scare him as much as it scared the Politburo. The *Renhai* might be one of the oldest ships in the Chinese fleet, but she was still a match all by herself for everything the Taiwanese and Philippinos could muster. Though China categorized her as a destroyer, with a hundred and twenty-two vertical missile silos, she carried as much lethality as any Western cruiser and was classified as a cruiser by NATO. The *Renhai* could pump enough death and destruction into the air in ten minutes to destroy every other surface combatant in the area.

As long as nobody invited the Americans and the Japanese into the fray.

Well, the unauthorized flight of a Kestrel into Chinese territory and out again had gotten everyone properly riled. He still wasn't authorized to shoot any missiles or even fire any warning shots with his 130mm gun, but his new instructions were perhaps better. He was to board the ships of the archipelago to find the kidnapped village.

Han shook his head in bemusement. A kidnapped village? Taken in broad daylight by a rocket ship? What kind of science-fiction fantasy was this, anyway? If he had not seen the space capsule descending with his own eyes, being shot at by fighter planes from China's Air Force, he would not have believed it.

He still didn't quite believe it, and he was uncomfortable with the idea that his nation had seen fit to shoot at a capsule loaded with hundreds of kidnapped Chinese citizens. Something did not ring true here.

What *did* ring chillingly true was the way the Brain-Trust had smacked down half a dozen Chinese fighter planes. His people were still studying the radar, infrared, and visuals from the battle, trying to ascertain exactly what had happened. The BrainTrust isle ships were supposed to be virtually defenseless, so something was very wrong here indeed. Perhaps the Politburo had shown wisdom beyond their normal standards in holding off on an assault all this time.

One thing was certain. A little caution was in order for this upcoming boarding action. Maybe even a lot of caution.

The lieutenant in charge of the boarding party stepped onto the *Taixue's* boat dock with a confident swagger. He had forty marines with him, five times more troops than the entire Fuxing fleet could muster, according to his briefing. Any firefights would be short and sweet.

Two BrainTrust peacekeepers, one a mere woman, stood on the dock to greet him, looking irritatingly unconcerned with his firepower.

But least concerned of all was the lithe Chinese girl with long shiny hair who stood with them, imperiously looking down her nose at him. "Where is your captain?" she demanded.

The officer stood very still, very erect. "The captain does not accompany boarding parties. I am in charge here."

The girl stepped into his personal space, challenging him. "You are confused. I am Liu Fan Hui, daughter of the

Politburo. These are my ships, Lieutenant. I require an audience with your captain."

The lieutenant controlled himself, holding back a biting response. Fighting with Red Princelings was contraindicated for those seeking career advancement. In the end he commed the *Renhai* and told the captain that Liu Fan Hui, daughter of the Politburo, demanded to speak with him. In person. Here. Now.

Once the captain had promised to comply, Fan relaxed. "You and your men are welcome to stay with me here on the dock till he arrives."

The lieutenant wisely chose to acknowledge this with a nod, since his verbal thank you might have sounded unrepentantly sarcastic.

Yet another boat arrived carrying the captain. After brief introductions, Fan started in on him, treating him no better than the lieutenant. "I understand you're here to search my ships for a kidnapped Chinese village. Do you realize how ridiculous that sounds?"

Captain Chunlan knew exactly how ridiculous it sounded. "Orders are orders, ma'am. And I got good visuals of the space capsule that came down here a few hours ago. It seems at least possible that such a kidnapping could have occurred."

Fan rolled her eyes. "Well, as you say, you have your orders." She turned and yelled, "Hey, Chen! You're up!"

Chen, the very incarnation of the pasty-faced geek who needed web-addiction rehabilitation, stumbled onto the deck. Fan introduced him. "This is Chen Ying, a son of the Politburo."

While Chunlan digested this, she pointed at the lieutenant and the two peacekeepers. "Take your men and divide them into three teams. Peacekeeper Sun will accompany one team, Security Chief Baddeley will accompany another, and Chen will accompany the lieutenant here with a third. Roam the ships as you will, but obey the peacekeepers, lest you wander into a nuclear reactor room and come out glowing in the dark. Or for that matter, just get so lost we have to send a team to find you."

The lieutenant spluttered, "I was planning to have twenty separate two-man teams. Even with twenty teams, there are an awful lot of passages and holds to inspect here."

Fan raised an eyebrow at him, then turned and raised her eyebrow even higher at the captain. Finally the captain growled, "Do as she says, Lieutenant."

"Aye, aye, Captain."

Moments later only Fan and the captain remained on the dock. For the first time, Fan relaxed and smiled, though danger still lurked in her eyes. "It was so good of you to come aboard, Captain. Since we seem to be sharing this part of the ocean on a somewhat permanent basis, I thought it would be well to have a meal together while our troops are inspecting the ships. I'll introduce you to the other members of my management team."

The captain gave her a baffled smile. "These are really your ships? These people are your employees?"

Fan tossed her hair impatiently. "Well, they might as well be, although they don't entirely realize it yet."

Captain Chunlan found dinner unexpectedly entertaining. For one thing, the food was excellent. Sure, he found a certain excessive emphasis on seafood, between the shrimp salad and the lobster bisque and the broiled kahala, but it was all fresh. The food on board the *Renhai* was adequate, but hardly in this category, no matter that his chef strove so mightily.

Try as he might, Han could not help being entertained by the story of the rocket ship that had invaded China's sovereign territory. It had taken much coaxing to get the story, but sitting at dinner in his elegant dress uniform, doing his best to look and sound harmless, the tale eventually came forth.

The spaceship had been launched by people far outside his jurisdiction, with neither consent nor even discussion with the local management. There had been no pilot. He had had thoughts of detaining that individual, but there was none. The lone woman who had been aboard as the rocket entered Chinese airspace was currently lost at sea.

He suspected the parachute that fell too fast from the capsule near the end had carried her. His sonar people had picked up some kind of bizarre sonic event as he approached her drop point, and a copter sent to investigate had found only blood and sharks. He warned his hosts what his men had found, urging them not to get their hopes up for finding her. The sanguinity with which they greeted his news suggested that a larger tale surrounded this woman. He would look in his briefing materials for information about a woman named Ping when he returned to his ship.

The captain tried to finagle a little data about possible fighter planes in the vicinity that might have shot up the Chinese jets as they zoomed around the spacecraft. On this, his hosts offered not one iota of information. He'd sent a copter to buzz the BrainTrust and look for signs of fighters on board; the only thing the copter had found suspicious was a blackened and burned helicopter pad, which his people surmised could have been caused by an F-35B, the VTOL version. But if an F-35 had been involved in the action, and if it had landed here, it was clearly now long gone—another item upon which he could take no action.

The direction of the conversation changed once more and could not be further diverted. He should have found the topic of this new unrelenting discussion tiresome, but the impassioned voice of the principal speaker gave it a certain verve.

Lenora Thornhill had clearly been born to teach. Whether she was one of the best teachers or one of the worst he had ever encountered remained undecided. "So as you can see, Captain, we can accelerate children, even children who would be considered unexceptional, through an educational process that will prepare them for the most challenging endeavors at far greater speed than the traditional teacher/classroom setup."

Captain Ainsworth interrupted, "Captain Chunlan, do you have children?"

Chunlan nodded. "A boy, twelve, and a girl, eight."

Lenora pounced. "How well is their education coming

along? Will they be able to get into the top universities China has to offer?"

The topic was a sore point for Han. "We are about to engage a tutor for my son. His grades are poor." He added a justification. "I am convinced he is bored."

Lenora snorted. "Of course he's bored! Either he's ahead of the class, in which case he needs more material, or he's behind, in which case he needs better cognitive scaffolding for the material already in hand. Either way, the best answer is a custom-tailored educational experience, the kind Accel can supply."

For a moment Fan Hui vibrated in her seat, making him think of the excited college kid she should have been rather than the…person…she seemed to have become. "Captain! Do you think you could bring your son here to the Fuxing for college preparatory work? I can personally vouch for the excellence of the materials, you know. In addition to being a lead investor and the onboard Politburo liaison, I am also a student here." Her enthusiasm spilled across the table. "You simply must bring him to us." She deflated a little as she looked at Lenora. "We *can* take him, can't we?"

Lenora chuckled. "We'd be delighted to have him here." She looked meaningfully at Han. "If the captain would allow him, of course. Our system's a bit nontraditional, Fan. Not everyone wants their children to experience something this radical."

Chunlan kept his expression impassive. He was now in a very tight spot. Letting his son go to school on the Fuxing would imperil his mission. If he needed to fire on the archipelago, could he do so knowing his son was here? On the other hand, could he really say no to this most determined, dangerous, and frightfully competent daughter of the Politburo who would one day be his unquestioned superior? He started to speak, still not sure what he would actually say, when his lieutenant charged into the room.

"Captain! None of the workers on these ships have their papers! But I am certain they are all hukou peasants!" He paused, his face shading into purple. "And they all have guns!"

Captain Ainsworth stood with a roar. "Nonsense! None of the children have guns, and the rest keep their guns locked in the armory except when we are at Condition Red Defense of Ship." He sat back down again. "Which is our current status, actually."

Captain Chunlan stared at Captain Ainsworth. "Your ship is at battle stations?"

Ainsworth shrugged. "Well, as much at battle stations as we can muster. It's not like we really have any battle stations worth manning." A glint in Ainsworth's eyes suggested this was not the entire truth, but enough for this discussion.

Chunlan prepared to shout back a bit himself, but Fan beat him to the punch. "Really, Captain Chunlan, what did you expect? You send forty heavily-armed soldiers to board us with no invitation or even a request, just an assertion that your troops will arrive in a few minutes. For a fleet with no professional fighting capacity beyond five peacekeepers, this constitutes an invasion with overwhelming force. Of *course,* Captain Ainsworth went to Condition Red. It demonstrates excellent initiative. It would be terrible if he had to consult me before performing his obvious duties."

Everyone was left speechless by this. Fan turned to the lieutenant. "And of course all my workers are hukou peasants. Why would I bring valuable urban workers to labor in my enterprises when peasants will do just fine?"

The lieutenant stuttered. "But…they have no papers!"

Fan waved her hand dismissively. "The captain probably has them locked in a safe somewhere. There's no need for them on these ships. No one cares."

This left the lieutenant gaping. It gave Captain Chunlan a moment's pause as well. Could it be that no one cared if they were hukou peasants? He couldn't quite wrap his head around the idea, but it made sense. The special privileges of the urban Chinese were irrelevant here. In fact, the irrelevance of those privileges—privileges *he* had—was not only an affront, but it was also…amusing in its own way.

The lieutenant recovered somewhat. "And they have guns!"

Fan Hui smiled angelically at Captain Chunlan as if the lieutenant did not exist. "Of course they have guns. They are descendants of the peasant army that fought so bravely for Chairman Mao. *'The guerrilla must move amongst the people as a fish swims in the sea.'* I'm sure you know this better than I, Captain."

The lieutenant spluttered again. "But…private citizens are not allowed to own firearms!"

Fan glared at him. "Really, you become tiresome. On the mainland, of course, private firearms are illegal. A necessary rule for the protection of the State. But here we are part of the BrainTrust, lieutenant. Our local rules reflect our local needs."

Captain Chunlan listened in amazement. This girl turned everything on its head! She was right, of course, about Mao. Peasant armies indeed! No one in the current Politburo would approve of private firearms today, of course—not even Fan's parents, he suspected—but in this place at this time Fan could stand on Mao's teachings and not even the Politburo would dare disagree openly.

The lieutenant would not give up. "Captain Chunlan, there are vidcams all over these ships. Presumably they have comprehensive recordings of everything that has happened in the last twenty-four hours. If we confiscate those recordings, we can stop this futile search and know for sure where the kidnapped villagers are."

For a moment the captain marveled at the lieutenant's determination. He moved on to envy the lieutenant's simplistic view of the situation. Sure, they could demand those recordings, but what would actually happen next? Looking at the stony faces of both the Fuxing Fleet Captain and the Mission Commander, he became quite certain that such a demand would lead to a most sincere Defense of Ship action.

Peasants were of course just peasants even if they had guns, but on this ship, they would be led by peacekeepers who, according to every briefing from every event that ever involved them, were so formidable as to yet be undefeated. Could his forty men take the ship in the face of such defiance? Where everyone but his own men knew every nook and cranny, every vantage point, every kill zone? How many hundreds of peasants lived on board these ships, anyway? He could hear Chairman Mao laughing at him across the ages. The lieutenant, with his unyielding focus on his mission, had placed his captain in an impossible position.

The thumping of Marine boots in the passageway saved Chunlan from answering. Everyone turned to watch.

Accompanied by two Marines who towered over her, an elderly woman shuffled into the room. Except she did not exactly shuffle; her feet moved as if shuffling, but she held her head high and smiled with gentle wisdom upon the captain.

A Marine spoke excitedly. "We found one of the kidnapped villagers, Captain."

The lieutenant pointed triumphantly. "There you have it!"

The elder looked at the lieutenant as if she were inspecting a bug. "My name is Nuan. My family and I have come here to help with the Fuxing's reef farming, and with Liu Fan Hui's mining venture."

Farming and mining. Exactly what peasants were supposed to do with their time. Somehow, Captain Chunlan suspected it didn't mean quite the same thing here with these BrainTrust people, but on paper it couldn't appear more proper.

The captain supposed it was now up to him to make some sense of this. "Were you kidnapped?"

Nuan snorted. "Not until your Marines here dragged me away from my quarters."

Chunlan looked to the marines. "Was there any evidence of kidnapping? Was she locked in her cabin, chained, or anything at all?" Of course back on the mainland, if a peasant were chained up to make sure he made it to work the next day, it would usually pass without comment. Still, the captain was here with specific orders to find kidnapping victims.

The Marines looked sheepish. "No, sir. She seemed free to come and go as she pleased."

The lieutenant croaked out an argument. "Where could she go to escape out here two hundred miles from home?"

The captain finally saw his way through to a survivable outcome. "Nuan, I have forty marines here able and willing to escort you and your family anywhere you'd like to go. Do you desire to come with us?"

Nuan glared at the Marines and the lieutenant, then once again turned her compassionate glow upon the captain. "We are happier here than we have been in two thousand years."

Whoa. Two thousand years. Who *was* this aged peasant, anyway? No matter.

Captain Chunlan rose. "Our task here is done. As I suspected, there are no kidnapped villagers."

The lieutenant opened his mouth to speak, but the captain silenced him with a look and turned to his hosts. "Mission Commander, Fleet Captain, Liu Fan Hui, this meal was lovely."

All rose, Fan swiftest, taking the lead as her training no doubt compelled her to. "And it was a delight to have you here, Captain. We should do this again." She had a thought. "Indeed, living in such close proximity, I believe we should make this a monthly gathering. To liaise, and make sure no failures in communication lead to hasty errors."

The captain nodded gravely.

Fan Hui reached into her pocket and pulled out a cell phone. "Take this," she urged, pushing the phone into his hand. "This is a BrainTrust phone. The most reliable thing you can use on the open ocean if there's an archipelago nearby."

The captain accepted the phone, which he knew was not only reliable but also quite invulnerable to prying ears. He wondered what he and Liu Fan Hui would find to talk about in such privacy, but "Thank you," was all he said.

He turned to Lenora. "I'll get back to you about my son. I must think about it."

Lenora nodded. "Any questions, just call." She smiled. "Use Fan's phone if you want to."

By the time Captain Chanlun reached his cruiser he already knew what he would do. First, he would inform the Politburo that the Fuxing held no kidnapped villagers. The vehicle that had invaded China's sovereign airspace had been destroyed, as you could see from the sensors on the *Renhai*. The lone woman who had been aboard during the incursion was lost at sea amid blood and sharks. Case closed.

He also knew he would send his son to Lenora, and probably his daughter as well. His decision had nothing to do with the politics of appeasing a petulant princeling, nor did it have anything to do with concerns about military tactical posture. It had only to do with the fact that Captain Han Chunlan was a father. His children deserved the best education they could get.

13

PRACTICAL ETHICS

For every challenge we face—unemployment, poverty, crime, income growth, income inequality, productivity, competitiveness —a great education is a major component of the solution.
    —Bruce Rauner

Jam caught up with Dash outside Lenora's classroom. Dash was just finishing a conversation on her phone. "Thank you, *Bu* Amanda. I understand how difficult it will be to move everyone, but we need the space. Should we consider building another full isle ship for medical research and medical tourism? I wouldn't be surprised if we could fill a whole ship soon." Dash listened for a moment. "Yes, quite right. Putting a medical ship with the Fuxing would be an excellent idea."

A few moments later, Dash said goodbye. She turned to Jam with a big smile. "I don't know how much you heard, but we are taking over the whole Wenara Wana Monkey Forest deck of the *Chiron* for rejuvenation patients."

"No more deaths?" Jam asked with concern.

"Not with the ones who pass our prescreening. We can scale up our treatments of them while separately figuring out how to treat the others."

Jam hugged her. "Congratulations." She pulled away. "Now, what did you want to see me about, here outside Lenora's classroom?"

"I have a gift for Professor Thornhill. I thought you should do the presentation." Dash handed Jam her tablet and explained what was so special.

Jam breathed a heavy sigh of relief. "Awesome. Thank you, girl."

They entered Lenora's sanctum together.

Lenora stood by the gaming table watching four youngsters hunch over a board. She looked up and smiled. "Jam." She left the children and met them halfway.

Jam performed the introductions. "Lenora, this is Dash. Dash, Lenora."

Lenora's smile grew wider. "Dash. I've heard so much about you."

Dash's smile seemed a little forced. "I seem to have trouble staying out of the limelight. But you know, it was Toni Shatzki who fought off the Chinese fighters and saved your people."

Lenora chuckled. "That's not the main reason everyone tells stories about you."

Jam intervened. "Anyway, Dash brought me this. You really need to see it." She synced the tablet to one of the wallscreens and started showing Lenora a series of short vid clips.

It only took Lenora a moment to understand what she was seeing. "Scenario testing. Instead of using the Milgram experiment with its risk of significant psychological trauma, the subject is shown a series of videos and stories, each of which requires a decision at the end. All the choices have both good and bad consequences, so it gives us rich feedback to evaluate. And of course, we would have the sensors hooked up to the subject while it's all happening."

Dash nodded. "Researchers had this all working quite well for identifying excellent leaders just after the turn of the century. The long-term payoff for using it was substantial, but so was the upfront cost. Poor leaders were unable to bring themselves to make the investment to groom the next generation of excellent leaders."

Dash paused. "You are not looking for excellent leaders, of course, or at least not exactly. But the principles are the same. And from what Jam tells me, you have the vision necessary to drive forward with it."

Lenora sighed. "One of my co-founders, James, tried to persuade me to use scenario testing like this instead of Milgram, but we weren't getting as reliable a read." She shook her head. "James hasn't talked to me since."

Dash spoke with confidence. "I am quite sure Dr. Caplan will be happy to speak with you again. I worked with him on this set of scenarios, which are better than what he had before. But even more important, I introduced him to Dark Alpha 42."

Lenora raised an eyebrow in puzzlement.

Jam explained. "It's this exotic AI Dash uses for analyzing really complex data. For some problems, it can give much better results than human interpretations."

Now Lenora looked excited. She clasped her hands as if in prayer. "And this Dark Alpha can interpret these scenarios? Better than we can? We don't have to use Milgram anymore?"

Dash beamed. "No Milgram anymore."

Lenora threw her arms around a surprised Dash. "Thank you!" Her voice broke. "You have no idea how much I've wanted this."

Jam added, "It gets better. Dash hooked it up to the camera in the cell phone. By watching for microexpressions, pupil dilation, and jittering from hand movement as the candidate watches the scenario, the new app can get a surprisingly good preliminary read."

Dash continued. "You can include this in the preliminary testing app, significantly improving candidate selection in the field, before they reach the Fuxing."

Lenora shook her head in amazement and looked at Jam. "So all the stories about her are true, then?"

Jam smiled wickedly at Dash. "*Almost* all of them."

"Hey!" Dash exclaimed, and glared back.

Dash fiddled with the instruments surrounding Ping's hospital bed. "Considering everything, you are in very good shape. I'll probably let you out of here tomorrow."

Ping responded enthusiastically. "Great! I think Captain

Jack is throwing a party tomorrow night. We'll go dancing!"

Dash rolled her eyes.

Jam stuck her head in the door. "If you're done, Dash, I have someone who needs to see Ping. In private."

Dash looked puzzled but obeyed the implicit request. She looked at Ping. "I'll see you in the morning if not before."

As she exited the room, an older Chinese couple stepped past her. Upon seeing Ping, the woman gasped; Ping growled, and Jam closed the door behind them.

Dash frowned. "Who are they?"

Jam's eyes gleamed. "Their names are Shu Shi and Kuo Lim. I met them in Baotong." She held her hand up to cup her ear as if trying to more clearly hear the sounds from Ping's room. "As for who they are, that is what I'm trying to find out."

The sounds rose and fell. Despair, anger, and something that might have been a muffled laugh reached them in quick succession. Finally, the door opened.

Shu Shi looked downcast, weeping openly. Her husband hugged her tightly. "Well, Ms. Jam, it was a good thought. Thank you for trying." Kuo Lim continued to hold her as they shuffled, despondent, down the hallway.

Then, as they were about to turn into a side passage, Shu Shi straightened and jumped up and down gleefully in her husband's arms. Kuo Lim looked back at Jam and spoke to her in a fierce whisper. Shu Shi looked back as well and slumped once more as they disappeared from view.

Dash twitched her nose, perplexed. "What was that all

about?"

Jam just shook her head, smiling slyly. "Looks like we have a winner."

After Dash departed to check on other patients, Jam went back into Ping's room.

Ping pursed her lips.

Jam raised her eyebrows innocently. "What?"

Ping sighed. "It's terrible, what happened to their family. Shame about their daughter."

Jam nodded sagely. "Evil. And tragic. But I have to wonder—"

Fan Hui strutted into the room. "Your name is Ping?"

Ping glared at the intruder. "What could *you* possibly want?"

"I'm Liu Fan Hui."

"I know who you are."

"Excellent." Fan pulled a small box from her pocket, removed a military medal, and placed it on Ping's pillow. "For you, for heroism in protecting the people of China. And just as importantly, protecting my personal workers."

Ping rolled her head to contemplate the medal. "You *do* know I shot down two Chinese fighters while protecting your workers, right?"

Fan waved it aside. "Following improper orders. Imagine shooting down a craft full of Chinese citizens! Insane." She scrutinized Ping's face. "Do I know you? You look familiar."

Ping started to pull a pillow over her face but thought

better of it. Instead, she glared at her interrogator. "I've spent most of my life in Chicago."

Fan frowned. "Still…" She brightened. "You're a hukou peasant, aren't you?" Her tone suggested the question was rhetorical.

Ping licked her lips. "I'm a BrainTruster."

Again Fan waved away the counterpoint; objections slid off her like rainwater on a duck. "I shall give you something else in addition to the medal." She paused, hoping to see some anticipation in her audience, but in this she was finally disappointed. "Urban papers."

Ping's eyes bulged. "You want to give me urban papers? But if I *were* a hukou peasant, that would be—"

"Not for me," Fan announced triumphantly. "I have persuaded my father to try another experiment. We shall be giving new papers to the very meritorious who have suffered from the hukou system. Just a few for now, but eventually…" she looked off into the distance, seeing a shining new vista of enlightenment, "eventually, perhaps as many as one in a thousand peasants will be lifted up and transformed into urban citizens."

At this point two interruptions occurred, in the forms of Dash and Lenora. Dash spoke first. "Ping, if you're going to have this many visitors tracking through here, we're going to have to set up a traffic circle."

Dash looked at Fan. "Can you continue this conversation tomorrow? Ping needs to rest."

Fan smiled lazily at Dash. "Of course." She turned and said goodbye to Ping. "I *know* I know you from somewhere. Don't worry, I'll figure it out."

As Fan left hearing range, Lenora muttered, "As many

as one in a thousand." She sighed. "Baby steps. Very tiny itty bitty baby steps."

Ping looked up at Jam. "We have to kill that bitch, you know. You *do* know we have to kill her, don't you?"

Jam jerked, startled. "She hasn't really done anything wrong." She looked at Lenora. "Has she?"

Lenora chuckled. "Very helpful so far, actually."

Ping sighed. "Fine. I'll kill the bitch." Seeing Dash frown, she added, "Not until she needs it." She looked down. "I guess."

Dash continued on her current mission. "Everybody out now. Like I said, Ping needs to rest."

Lenora held up her hand, like a student in a classroom wishing to ask a question. "One last quick thing, please."

When Dash reluctantly nodded, Lenora turned to Ping. "I just got a call from Ciara. She says a young man just showed up requesting a place on the Prometheus, and that her doctors have never seen anyone so battered who was still alive. He has two kinds of tropical fevers, he's been stabbed at least twice and shot at least once, and if he'd arrived a day later he would've lost an eye to some kind of jungle parasite. He says he walked from Somalia, his name is Abshir, and he insisted we talk to you. He says you promised."

Ping went off in a flight of nearly hysterical laughter. "Ohmigod, he's in even worse shape than I was when…"

Jam took a step closer to her. "When?" she encouraged her friend.

Ping turned to Lenora. "By all means, tell Ciara to let him on board. He's more than earned it. Tell her it's all about the grit."

Ping glanced at Jam, who started to speak again. Ping squeezed her eyes shut and quickly interjected, "I'm very tired now. I need to rest."

Jam put her hands on her hips. "But—"

Dash put *her* hands on *her* hips. "Later."

Jam looked at Dash; Dash looked back; Jam slumped. "Well, it was worth a try." Together, Jam, Dash, and Lenora left Ping in solitude.

The mayor of Baotong forced himself to be very polite to the very powerful man on the other end of the phone. "Yes, sir, I understand, sir. I have some promising possibilities among the younger people in a village farther west. Have I considered giving the people who come to work the fields a higher percentage of revenues? But… Yes, sir. I, ah, yes, I'll be considering that too. Yes, sir. Thank you, sir." The mayor slammed the antique phone down.

His lunch break was coming to a close, and soon he'd be out in the field. Plowing.

For just a moment he regretted never studying the ridiculous machines the villagers cobbled together. He was now realizing that they'd saved an incredible amount of time using devices held together with duct tape and baling wire.

Well, soon this was all going to be nothing but a bad memory. A few days after his village had been kidnapped he'd received a new cell phone by special delivery. The sender was a mystery.

Puzzling over it, he'd flipped the phone on, despite

knowing that no cell phones worked here. But wonder of wonders, it hooked right up to the web and the cell system with not a hiccup. And it opened up an amazing world of opportunities for him.

He had been incredibly fortunate to be immediately contacted by a Russian oligarch who needed fast cash so he could move his funds out of the country before the Premier locked them down.

It had taken just about every penny the mayor had, but this morning the oligarch had assured him that they'd gotten the funds out in the nick of time. Soon the oligarch would start paying him back, with interest. A lot of interest. Then the mayor would move away from this cursed place just like the villagers, only a lot richer.

Meanwhile, in his favorite game app, *Peasant Crush*, he only needed two more aquamarine gems to level up. He could probably play for a few minutes now before going out into the fields. Yes, just a few minutes.

Matt was sitting in the *Haven*'s ultra-plush cafeteria savoring a luxurious cup of hot chocolate when Gina slipped into the seat next to him. He smiled at her like a starstruck college boy.

She made fish lips at him. "Love it when you look at me like that."

They sat together, sipping their drinks, comfortably at home with each other.

Eventually Matt broke the silence. "Finally outsmarted them."

Gina raised an eyebrow. "BrainTrust?"

Matt popped both eyebrows up and down in a quick acknowledgment.

Gina smirked. "Unlikely."

Matt shook a finger at her. "Skeptic."

Gina waited patiently.

"Bought a seat in the Consortium for SpaceR. Next time they soak me when I need a rush job, I'll be on the profiting side of the deal."

Gina chuckled. "Brilliant. I'm sure they all appreciate how they've been outmaneuvered." She kissed his cheek. "No one can outfox you for long, darling."

Lenora came to the teamwork table where three of her best and brightest had set forth on a mysterious project. She was just thrilled with this team-up: a sixteen-year-old girl from Baotong, a fourteen-year-old computer prodigy from Canton, and a seventeen-year-old from the deserts near Mongolia. Kids from such different backgrounds coming together to do...something. "So, folks, what's this secret project you're working on?"

The boy from Canton looked away guiltily. The boy from Mongolia pursed his lips and started tapping furiously on his tablet, looking for something. The Baotong girl just smiled and answered. "We're conducting an intervention for the mayor of Baotong."

Lenora kept her smile fixed in place. "An intervention? For the mayor? As in, some sort of a virtual scenario game?"

The girl looked puzzled. "For reals, of course."

Lenora thought about commending the girl on the speed with which she was picking up American slang, then thought better of it.

The serious seventeen-year-old found what he sought on his tablet. "He's a tyrant."

The fourteen-year-old chimed in. "Level six on the ten point scale."

Lenora's eyes bulged. "There's a scale?"

The seventeen-year-old stood and showed her his tablet. "See, right here in the module we're studying, there's a table for rating tyrants."

Lenora studied the screen. Yes, the mayor was a level-six tyrant, employing every technique up to, but not including, rape, murder, kidnapping, and torture. If he hadn't worked as an underling for even worse tyrants, he would have scored a seven.

The girl explained further. "So according to the module, here's the list of techniques it's ok to use to neutralize him. As you can see, they all require his cooperation, more or less."

Lenora looked at her in puzzlement. "But we already neutralized him. Everyone who worked for him came here."

The girl shook her head. "If we don't intervene, he'll just do the same things again to another village, a village of people less able to protect themselves. He still has money and political favor." Her smile developed a tiger's edge. "Well, he had money until yesterday."

Lenora had a sinking feeling. "Nigerian hoax?"

The seventeen-year-old waxed poetic. "It worked just

the way Accel said it would. Really sweet. It's quite fortunate he didn't get any Accel training, or I doubt we could have pulled it off."

Lenora stood stiffly. She would have to think about what was happening here very carefully. Best not to stomp on them in haste, however. They certainly had a point about the mayor.

There was, however, another problem. "So what are you planning to do with the money?" Lenora braced herself in preparation to offer stern words about people who plan to throw big parties.

Once again the girl answered. "We'll invest it in the Scholars' Loan program."

Lenora took back the harsh thoughts she'd prepared. "That will help a lot of good people."

The seventeen-year-old pointed at the girl. "That's what *we* thought. It was her idea."

Lenora smiled at the girl, who added, "And we expect, in the long run, to average a twelve percent return on the investment."

The fourteen-year-old interrupted. "Fourteen. Over the long run, fourteen percent."

Lenora stood frozen for a moment. Then she looked more closely at the module they had shown her, with the tyrant rating system and the ethically allowable responses.

How had he gotten this past the module vetting process? James would not have helped him, would he?

No matter. Her hands shook the tablet so hard her knuckles turned stark white. "Dmitri!"

I'd like to say a few words about inevitability. When an author fleshes out his characters and situations adequately, he sometimes finds himself fighting with his own creations over the direction of the story. Sometimes the author has to win, but sometimes it's best to let the characters have their way, especially if they're journeying to the key milestones anyway—just in a different way than anticipated.

Sometimes the situations and the people make things inevitable. A striking example in the BrainTrust is the subplot around Dmitri. I did not know it at the time, but Dmitri's character and story were inevitable from the moment I concluded that, because of costs, every person on the Brain Trust would have a cabin the same itty bitty size as everybody else.

How can that be? Well, let us consider the sequence of steps, each of which, in retrospect, had to happen.

Given that all the original cabins were tiny, and given that the BrainTrust regularly produced new billionaires, it was inevitable that some of those billionaires would get together and build a new isle ship just for themselves, where you could have any size residence as long as you could pay for it.

Of course, a ship just for billionaires in the world's most innovative locale offering the last word in creative tax havens would become one of the world's most prestigious residences.

Of course, a Russian oligarch would buy a place in this most prestigious place. Enter Dmitri.

Of course, the Russian Premier would compel Dmitri to kidnap Dash.

Of course, Dmitri would fail.

Of course, the Premier, being based on a real-life dictator who does this in real life, would assassinate him with polonium.

Of course, Dmitri would ask Dash for help.

Of course, Dash would save him.

And of course, Colin being Colin, he would put the recovered polonium in a vial for him.

Is the story of Dmitri finished? I hardly think so. What is the next inevitable step in his journey?

Of course, if I do my job correctly, then in the final climactic chapter of the final climactic book, when Dmitri's subplot twists to its final climactic conclusion, perhaps you will agree with me on the following:

It was never obvious. Yet it was indeed always inevitable.

The Braintrust - A Harmony of Enemies (1)

The Braintrust: A Crescendo Of Fire (2)

The Braintrust: Rhapsody for the Tempest (3)

Valentina
(Hugo Award Finalist)

David's Sling
(Prometheus Award Finalist)

EarthWeb

The Gentle Seduction (anthology)